THE LEGEND OF
SHADOW MOUNTAIN

Samantha Wolf Mysteries

Book 8

TARA ELLIS

ISBN-13:978-1547050635
ISBN-10:1547050632
The Legend of Shadow Mountain

Models: Breanna Dahl, Janae Dahl, Chloe Hoyle
Photographer: Tara Ellis Photography

NOTE FROM THE AUTHOR

I have to admit that I had a lot of fun writing The Legend of Shadow Mountain! This story is a little more intense than the others, with lots of action. I hope you get caught up in it as much as I did!

I would like to point out that while Ketchikan, the Alaska Boundary Range, and the Tlingit people all exist, Shadow Mountain and the legend are a result of my imagination. Taquka-ak is a real word for the Kodiak, and the local culture is rich with their own legends that surround it. Look it up!

This story is dedicated to all you adventurers. May you never stop dreaming of the mountains and the mysteries that they hold.

SAMANTHA WOLF MYSTERIES

Find these and Tara's other titles on her author page at Amazon!

amazon.com/author/taraellis

CONTENTS

1

A BIRTHDAY
SURPRISE

"Listen up! I need you all to gather 'round for an announcement!" Lisa Covington claps her hands for emphasis, much the same way she does for her seventh grade health class. Except that she's in her home at Covington Ranch, rather than the middle school. "Sam!" she exclaims with some frustration. "Could you please put Rocky outside and come join us?"

Samantha Wolf looks towards where her poodle is pawing at the backdoor. Torn between either following Lisa's orders or helping herself to another bowl of pudding, she sighs and puts the dish down. One thing she's learned this past year is to *not* make her teacher and friend ask her to do something twice.

Cassy laughs at Sam's distress before scooping up the last of the pudding and rushing into the formal sitting room. She joins the small crowd of friends and family jockeying for the limited seats.

Sam shakes her head as she watches the other girl go. Lisa is Cassy's older sister. She'll likely give her a disapproving look for eating the dessert on the cream-colored couch. At least Sam will be spared *that* reprimand. Closing the sliding glass door behind the newest edition to the Wolf family, she turns just in time to side step a shove from her older brother, Hunter.

"Ack!" he snorts while skidding to a stop short of the glass door. "You're getting fast, sis," he says almost approvingly. But then quickly covers up the praise with a tug at her ponytail. "But not quite fast enough!"

Sam half-heartedly swats her brother's hand away. She accepted the fact a long time ago that she was destined to be his primary target for constant teasing. Their three-year-old twin sisters are still too young to pick on. At fifteen, Hunter is only three years older than she is, but he's constantly pointing it out. He drives her crazy, but for all his torment, he's often there for her when she really needs him.

"Come on, Sam!"

Sam is pulled from her thoughts by the sound of her best friend's voice. Allyson Parker is seated on the nearest couch, patting urgently at the space beside her. Her bright red, curly hair is pulled up into an unruly bun, which is framed by a sparkly birthday crown. Sam placed the crown there herself earlier in the day at the local bowling alley.

Their small town of Oceanside doesn't have much for entertainment, but the old bowling alley is still a favorite venue for both young and old. Ally didn't hesitate when choosing the location for her thirteenth birthday. She invited a group of friends from school and they spent that Saturday afternoon bowling and playing games in the old-fashioned arcade. Lisa offered to host a more private dinner for family and close friends in her large estate. It's situated on the hill above Ally and Sam's more modest homes.

Sam rubs absently at her wrist as she hurries to sit down. While she's the tallest of her three friends, and more solidly built than Ally, she's nowhere near as good at bowling.

I really should have stopped with that third round, she thinks, plopping onto the cushion. Pushing at her overgrown bangs, she does her best to pull the loose strands of her long brown hair back into a pony. Her unusual green eyes are a stark contrast to Ally's blue. Their differences are more than skin-deep, with Sam being the more daring of the two, but it's part of what makes their friendship work so well.

They've been neighbors and friends for years, while Cassy was recently brought into the fold at the beginning of the school year. The olive-skinned girl was a crucial part of one of their most challenging mysteries, involving the previously abandoned Covington Ranch and a missing jewel. Sam ultimately helped reveal that Lisa is Cassy's half-sister, and with the location of the family gemstone uncovered, they've been able to restore the old horse ranch to its previous glory.

Cassy was living with her ailing grandmother, and welcomed the invitation to live with Lisa. Now, Sam can't imagine what it would be like without the outspoken girl in their lives.

Kathy Wolf steps up next to Lisa, and surveys the faces. "Are we all here?"

Sam glances across the room at her brother. Hunter raises his eyebrows questioningly back at her. It seems odd that their mother would be joining Lisa for an announcement. It's Ally's birthday, and they're in Cassy's house. They already gave Ally her birthday gift earlier; a nice hiking backpack to use on their next camping trip together.

Shrugging her shoulders, Sam can't help but throw in a parting expression in response to the earlier hair tugging. Scrunching up her nose and sticking her tongue out, she stops when she notices John is watching the exchange from his spot next to Hunter. John is Ally's big brother, and the oldest of their group at sixteen. With his tall stature and blonde hair, you would never guess he and Ally are related, if it weren't for their same shade of blue eyes.

Although he smiles crookedly at her, Sam blushes and tries to cover her face by pretending to cough. He has a way of making her feel immature. As if it weren't already bad enough being the youngest of the five, both Cassy and Hunter had birthdays the month before. Now, even her best friend is older than she is. Sam won't turn thirteen until next month, at the end of May.

Ally and John's parents silently step in behind the other two women, so that the four adults are now facing the five, seated kids. Sam and Ally exchange a look of alarm. It's beginning to feel like an ambush.

"First, I'd like to thank you all for letting me be a part of this special occasion," Lisa begins. "I would have never imagined that coming back to Oceanside for a teaching job would end with me discovering I had a sister, *and* getting the farm back!"

Kathy Wolf and Elizabeth Parker each put an arm around Lisa's shoulders and give her an affirmative hug. The three have become quite close over the past six months.

Sam relaxes a little, since the mood is obviously positive. She's suffered so many lectures due to her inquisitive nature, that she's always expecting the worst. However, something is definitely up. It's clear that their parents are plotting something.

"We know that you all have some different things planned for spring break this coming week," Kathy states, taking a step forward. "Our family was looking forward to seeing Ethan. The kids dad has been gone fishing in Alaska now for several months. Other than a few days at Christmas, that is."

Sam's throat catches at the word 'was'. Turning to look worriedly at Hunter, she forgets all about being mad at him. The scowl on his face is evidence enough that he's noticed their mom's choice of words, too.

Their father has worked as a commercial fisherman for most of Sam's life, but recently, he's taken on a bigger role in the large operation. Instead of working his normal four months out of the year, he's spent the past six months in Alaska, with only a few breaks in between the seasons. It's meant a much-needed increase in the family's income, but Sam doesn't think it makes up for not getting to see her dad every day.

Tears spring to her eyes at the thought of not getting to see him, and she instantly chastises herself for being so sensitive. Sam hates to cry in front of anyone. The fact that Ally reaches out and squeezes her hand only confirms that her distress is evident to everyone there, and she fights to choke back the strong emotions.

"Well, you kids are going to have to clear your calendar," Kathy rushes to add, not dragging the moment out any longer. "Something came up at the fishing village your dad is at, so he's going to have to stay over and help get things ready for the Chinook run." Putting her hands up to ward off any comments, she then makes a calm-down gesture and smiles at their confusion. "Ethan's boss, Mr. Stiles, happens to own a small float-plane business in Ketchikan, near the fishing village. He's offered to fly me and our kids up for the week!"

Sam's spirit soars at the news, but it's quickly followed by confusion. "Why do *all* of us need to 'clear our calendars'?" she asks, looking first at her mom and then at her friends. They all appear just as perplexed as she is.

"Because," Kathy continues, "I would never take the twins on a float plane to Alaska, for the same reason I have them napping right now in the other room. I can think of about a hundred other things I would rather do."

"And that means," Elizabeth Parker adds, looking meaningfully at John, Ally, and then Cassy, "that there are three extra seats on the plane."

It takes a moment for the full meaning to sink in. John is the first to figure it out, and he literally leaps from his chair. "We're going to Alaska?" he asks his voice incredulous.

Sam is so excited; she doesn't know what to do first. Ally immediately crushes her with a big hug and then Cassy joins them.

"Do you really mean it, Mom?" Ally squeals, nearly falling off the couch in a heap of arms and legs.

Laughing, Lisa claps her hands again, but this time it's with happiness at the success of their surprise. "We've all discussed it at length," she says loud enough to be heard over the celebrating. "And we agreed that since it's a short trip with Mr. Wolf waiting for you on the other end, that we're all okay with it. Plus," she adds, pointing at John. "We know you'll keep a close eye on everyone for us." As she speaks, Lisa turns to look specifically at Sam.

Sinking back involuntarily into the plush couch under the scrutiny, a small spark of apprehension stirs deep in Sam's stomach. Her dad has told her all about the amazing mountains and forest that surrounds the village, thick with both wild life and ancient beliefs. How can she avoid exploring *there*? Determined to stay out of trouble, Sam vows to be on her best behavior.

But she can't imagine a better place to find a mystery.

2

ALASKA OR BUST

As the group approaches the dock, the excitement among them is tangible. It's a rare spring day in the Pacific Northwest. The deep blue sky and cheery sun are almost enough to make them forget about the long, grey winter days.

Sam eyes the floatplane bobbing ever so slightly on the water. It's not as big as she thought it would be. They had all debated its size on the drive up. They didn't have far to go, since they're leaving from an area just north of Bellingham, less than an hour from their small town on the Washington State coast. They're close to the Canadian border here, so it's pretty much a straight-shot to Ketchikan, which is located in the southern-most end of Alaska, in a cluster of islands.

Sam tugs at the straps of her backpack, pulling it snug against her shoulders, which keeps it from bobbing while she walks. They were told to pack light and to expect sparse lodgings. Her sleeping bag roll is tied to the bottom of her pack, making a nice, evenly balanced load. Watching Cassy struggle to carry both her tote bag and full-sized sleeping gear, Sam is thankful she already had the camping equipment.

"Rocky, heel!" Sam tugs at the leash she has a firm grip on, reminding her strong-willed poodle that he needs to walk beside her, not in front. She adopted him from the local shelter a couple of months ago, but he settled right into their family as if he'd always been there. She was surprised when her dad suggested that she bring him along. He hasn't met Rocky yet, and apparently, dogs are welcome in the small village, *and* on floatplanes.

Hunter steps past Sam and catches Cassy's bag as it slips off her shoulder, and she gives him a crooked smile. "Guess I'm not so good at this 'packing light' thing." She nods at his pack as she speaks. It's similar in style to Sam's, but a little larger.

John has a full-on trek pack, with a spot on both the top and bottom for a sleeping roll and tent. He's been a scout for years, and is an avid outdoorsman. Since they obviously don't need a tent, he instead has Ally's sleeping bag tied on with his own. He turns to look back at his sister, who's walking alongside Sam, and shakes his head.

Last night, they'd had a lengthy debate about what to bring. They were given such short notice about the surprise trip, that they quickly threw everything together right before bed. John thought that Ally should use the new backpack Sam got her for her birthday, but Ally insisted on using her larger tote bag, similar to Cassy's.

"Let it go!" Ally demands now, glaring at her brother. Struggling to move the large strap of her bag over to her other shoulder, she does her best to keep up with the others. John often accuses her of being 'high maintenance', a label she despises. While it's true that she enjoys her expansive wardrobe, and spends much more time getting ready in the morning than Sam does, she certainly isn't prissy. She simply couldn't figure out a way to shove her sandals, hiking boots, *and* clothing for three days into such a small pack! Glancing over at Sam, she admires her friend's ability to be comfortable in the same worn blue jeans and t-shirt for more than a day.

"Is that our plane?" Cassy gasps. She's the first to reach the end of the dock, and nervously watches as her sister steps up to shake the hand of a man who's leaning against the side of the yellow aircraft.

"Since this is the only plane hanging around," Hunter replies with a heavy dose of sarcasm, "I'm going to take a *wild* guess and say 'yes'."

Punching her brother's shoulder, Sam pushes around him and throws an arm around Cassy's shoulders. "I'm sure it's perfectly safe, Cass," she says reassuringly casting a stern look at Hunter. "My dad would never send it for us if it weren't."

Rolling his eyes, Hunter waves the girls off and moves over to speak in low tones with John. Although they're close in age, the younger boy is quite a bit shorter. Sam got her father's height, while Hunter tends to take after their mom's slight stature. But he has the same dark hair and eyes of his dad, so he's still hopeful that he might have another growth spurt.

"Are you Mr. Watchman?" Lisa asks with her hand clasped in a firm grip.

Nodding slowly, the pleasant-looking man flashes a bright smile. "Call me Tulok." Stepping back so he can take in the whole group, he then absently rubs at his chin. "We'll have a pretty full load." Kneeling down, he extends a hand to Rocky. The cinnamon colored poodle happily steps up to receive a scratch behind the ear.

"It's okay to bring him?" Sam asks nervously. She would hate to leave him behind.

"I'm sure he'll make a fine passenger," Tulok laughs while straightening and turning to Sam.

His dark features and angular cheekbones make his native heritage apparent, but the middle aged man doesn't have an accent. All Sam knows is that the original people of Alaska are referred to as Inuit, but there are multiple groups among them. Her dad said that the pilot was born and raised in the fishing village that he's stationed at, and she's looking forward to questioning him about the area during the plane ride.

"I'm guessing you're Sam. Your father

mentioned you'd be bringing Rocky, and you have his eyes." Winking, he turns back to Lisa. "Thank you for escorting them this far, Miss Covington. I assure you that I will safely hand them off to Mr. Wolf this afternoon."

Without any further conversation, Tulok opens the only door on the side of the plane, and waves at them all to begin boarding. They each hug Lisa before climbing the drop-down steps and disappearing into the bullet-shaped plane.

Sam pauses at the threshold as her eyes adjust to the sudden change in light, and as she then moves forward, she's surprised to see that a woman and small child are already seated at the front of the plane.

"Hello!" the young mother calls out cheerfully. Her blonde hair is pulled back into a ponytail, and her bright blue eyes sparkle with excitement. "I'm Kerry, and this is my son, Riley. We're going to visit my husband at the village. Is this your first time on one of these? I've never been on a floatplane, and I seriously can't w*ait* to go!"

Kerry is nearly bouncing in her seat with her last exclamation, and Sam instantly likes her. "I'm

Sam, and no, I've never been on one and I'm super excited, too!" There are eight seats in the main body of the plane, with four rows, one to each side. It creates a narrow walkway in the middle and Sam turns to make her way to the seat opposite her new friend.

"How old is Riley?" Sam works at shoving her backpack under her seat as she asks the question.

"Three. I hope he does okay. It's his first time flying." Ruffling the young boy's hair that's the same color as his mother's, Kerry lifts him onto her lap. "Tulok said I need to belt him in with me for the take-off and landing, but then he's free to roam. I'm guessing he's going to spend most of the trip harassing your dog!"

As if on cue, Riley stretches his small hands out for Rocky, who took up a spot in the isle between the seats. Nosing forward, the friendly dog licks at the young boys fingers, causing a squeal of delight.

"Oh, he's adorable!" Ally exclaims, grabbing the empty seat behind Sam.

Cassy sits across from her, behind Kerry. "He would have fun playing with your sisters,

Sam," she adds. Her tote bag won't fit under the seat, so she awkwardly arranges her feet on top of it, and then laughs at Ally who is forced to sit the same way.

"Give me the luggage that won't fit." Tulok is standing in the open door with his hands out, and promptly disappears with first John's pack, and then comes back to take the other three. The sound of another door slamming at the far end of the plane indicates the presence of a cargo area.

John settles in behind his sister, shoving Hunter playfully into the final seat available. He feigns injury, grabbing at his chest, but then promptly pops his head up next to Cassy's. "Got any food?" he begs. Smiling widely at the beef jerky she pulls out of her sweatshirt pocket, he then grimaces. "What's it going to cost me?"

"Silence," Cassy answers without hesitation. Tucking her straight black hair behind her ears, she stares at him with her dark eyes. "You can't tease me the *whole* flight. If you do, I get dibs over you on the bunks when we get there."

Scrunching his brows together in serious contemplation, Hunter finally nods. "It'll be tough, but worth it. Deal."

Grinning at her victory, Cassy hands over a large piece of the jerky. She would have given it to him anyway. The two share a unique ability to eat constantly but never get full, *or* gain weight. She was pretty scrawny when she first became friends with Sam and Ally, because of her rough living conditions with her grandma. While she's managed to get to a healthier weight since moving in with Lisa, she's still on the slim side.

Tulock suddenly jumps back in the door, and stands silhouetted by the bright sunlight behind him. "Are you all settled?" he asks, looking at each of them. When everyone shouts yes, he claps his hands approvingly. After securing the hatch, he swiftly moves up the isle with practiced ease, even stepping over Rocky without breaking stride. Once at the open area between the seats and cockpit, he turns back and clears his throat, preparing for his pre-flight speech. "My name is Tulock Watchman, and I have the pleasure of being your pilot today. We'll be flying into a small coastal village, just north of Ketchikan, Alaska. This craft is a Havialland, DHC – 3 Otter, with a max capacity of ten occupants, a top speed of 160 mph, max height of 18,000 feet, and a range of 945 miles. We should reach our destination in under five hours, with clear skis and no rain in the forecast. Any questions?"

"Umm … ," Cassy says hesitantly. "Have you ever crashed?"

Sam expects Tulock to laugh at the question, but instead, he turns a very serious eye on her friend. "No, I have not. But several of my friends have. Floatplanes have gotten a bad reputation over the years, but most of the incidents were due to flying in spite of poor weather conditions. This will not be a factor for us today, young lady, so sit back and enjoy the ride." Smiling again the pilot nods once and abruptly turns away from them. After hitting some overhead switches and grabbing a set of earphones hanging from a peg in the ceiling, Tulock swings into the pilot seat and deftly makes the twin engines roar to life.

Not sure how she should take the statement, Sam glances back at Ally, and then John. While Ally is looking a bit pale, John has a wide grin on his face. Reaching forward to squeeze his sister's shoulder reassuringly, he then winks at Sam.

"This should be a lot of fun," he comments, having to speak loudly to be heard over the increasing volume. "I did some reading last night before turning in. These planes are the most common form of transportation up there. We'll be fine."

Turning back around as a deep vibration starts to fill the space around her; Sam can't help but feel a strong sense of impending danger.

3

TAQUKA-AQ

Sam rubs at her temples to ease the pressure, and is finally able to take a deep breath. Now that they're at what Tulock calls cruising altitude, the engine noise has leveled off and her stomach has stopped doing flip-flops. Sam's never been on a floatplane before, so she isn't sure what's considered a normal take-off. Although it was smooth, it felt like the most extreme rollercoaster ride she's ever been on!

Whimpering slightly, Rocky nudges at her hand to get her attention. Looking down into the soft brown eyes of her poodle, Sam laughs aloud at his concerned expression. Having pulled him onto her lap for the take-off, she didn't realize how tight she was holding him. Forcing herself to relax, she soothingly rubs his back.

"It's okay, buddy," she coos. Not convinced, he leans forward and lays his head on her shoulder in what Sam calls his 'doggy hug' posture. Wrapping her arms back around him in a gentler embrace this time, she whispers encouraging words into his ear.

"Doggy!" Laughing, Riley claps his hands and then points again at Rocky. Seemingly undisturbed by the experience of riding in the floatplane, the youngster is only interested in the dog.

Ears perking, Rocky jerks his head off Sam's shoulder and turns happily towards the little boy. Leaping from her lap, he joins his friend in the small isle, where he wags an eager tail in anticipation of the attention he's going to get.

Looking up from the cute scene, Sam meets Kerry's eyes. "He's already used to lots of noise and hair-tugging," she explains. "I have twin sisters the same age as Riley."

Nodding in understanding, Kerry looks pleased. "Well, he's the perfect distraction! It looks like I was all worried for no reason. Who are you going to visit?" the young woman asks, turning to include all five kids in her question.

"Our dad is kind of in charge of the guys going on the Salmon trollers next week," Sam answers, gesturing towards Hunter.

"Oh! Your dad is Mr. Wolf?"

"Yeah!" Ally answers for them, leaning forward over the back of Sam's seat. "My name is Ally. Cassy and I are Sam's best friends, and John is my brother." She points at Cassy and John as she speaks. "We all got to come along since it's spring break, and Sam's mom didn't want to take the twins."

"Well, I certainly can't blame her for that!" Kerry agrees. "I almost didn't come, either. I can't imagine bringing two little ones."

"Have you been there before?" John asks. Scooting out into the isle so he can hear everyone better, he gets down on his knees and moves up in between Ally and Cassy.

"No." Shaking her head, Kerry's ponytail bobs. "This is the first season my husband has gone out on a troller. He normally hauls crab, but it's supposed to be a good salmon run this year. He said the village is nice, but I guess there's been some tension lately between the locals and the fishermen."

Sam is surprised to hear about the trouble, especially with her dad in charge. One of the reasons his boss, Mr. Stiles, promoted him is because of his ability to get along well with everyone. Is that why he couldn't come home for the week? She knows that her dad wouldn't say anything to them about it. It really isn't any of their business. Remembering that Tulock is from the village, Sam peeks over and confirms that he has turned his head slightly, obviously listening to the conversation. Cringing, Sam wishes she could stop the discussion. If there really *is* some sort of conflict, the last thing her dad needs is for them to gossip about it in front of Tulock.

"Did something happen to cause it?" Cassy asks innocently, unaware of Sam's negative reaction to the question.

"Perhaps I can answer that for you," Tulock offers, his voice not indicating any sort of irritation. "It may help ward off any misunderstandings."

Relieved that Tulock intervened, Sam is still wary. Talking about it without her dad present doesn't feel right. But since Kerry brought it up, it'll be better to have their guide dispel any rumors. Sam's mom is always challenging them to evaluate where, when, and with whom they are discussing something. It's saved her from damaging friendships, and when it comes to her dad, she's extra cautious.

Having removed his headset shortly after take-off, and now with an open, blue sky spread out before them, Tulock turns in his seat to face them. His expression is relaxed, and if the topic is a touchy one, his demeanor doesn't hint at it.

"The history of my people, the Tlingit (pronounced kleen-kit), is ripe with legends. Especially involving animals, since it is believed that they are people who have passed and shape-shifted to their new forms."

Sam is both surprised and fascinated. While not at all what she expected to hear, she leans forward eagerly. Legends and myths are the perfect foundation for a good mystery!

"I don't get it," Hunter interjects. Pushing himself up from where he was reclined and chewing on another big piece of jerky, he leans out into the aisle. "Shape-shifted like Animorphs or something?"

"Hunter!" John scolds, smacking his friend on the arm. "Don't make light of it. There are several cultures who believe that animals are, or were people."

Hunter starts to defend himself, but Tulock chuckles and waves them both off. "No offense taken. Like every civilization, our people have evolved over thousands of years to our current state of beliefs. There are those of us who have embraced the new view of the world, some who chose to live by the old standards, and then the rest of us, who see things in a combination of the two. While there are many differences, some things do not waver. In my village, one such thing is the legend of Shadow Mountain."

"Oh! A legend!" Ally gasps. While Ally tends to be the more cautious of the three girls, she wouldn't change any of the excursions she's been on with Sam over the years. Although often reluctant, she shares in the same excitement when presented with another possible adventure. For Sam, just about anything can be a potential quest.

Sam shares a knowing smile with Ally and Cassy before turning back to Tulock. Though she's as curious as her friends are, she can't imagine how this has anything to do with her father.

"Our village sits on the shore of the Archipelago, a three-hundred mile chain of more than a thousand islands. The dense rainforest of the Alaska Boundary Range forms a mountainous wall from north to south. Shadow Mountain is a part of this, and rises directly behind us. It is protected by the Taquka-aq, the Kodiak bear. My people have passed on the story of Taquka-aq from generation to generation. It is a traditional tale that can only be presented by an elder. Perhaps you will have an opportunity to hear it while you are with us. I can tell you that the Kodiak visited my ancestors in her human from on many occasions, warning them not to hunt there, not to build shelters there, and to leave the gold at the heart of the mountain when the miners came through in the 1800s on their way to the Klondike. When her warnings are not honored, disaster often falls on those who commit the act, or our village is punished by the Taquka-aq."

"How is it punished?" Cassy nearly whispers caught up in the story.

"Two weeks ago," Tulock continues after turning briefly to look over the controls on the plane. "One of the men from your fathers group took it upon himself to explore the region that had been clearly stated as off limits. Our village is always happy to host men and women who chose to fish the waters with us, but we ask for the respect of our culture. Unfortunately, Like many before him, the lure of rumored gold drew him in."

"Gold?" Sam can't help but think of the last time she and Ally got involved in lost gold. It ended well, but things got quite dangerous first. While the small flame of excitement is spreading a warmth through her chest, Sam is guarded. She promised her mom to be on her absolute best behavior, and that means *not* chasing after gold. *Especially* if it's the cause of the trouble in the village and would bring the wrath of Taquka-aq.

4

INTO THE WILDERNESS

"There have been many that have tried to find the gold of Shadow Mountain, and all have failed," Tulock continues. He knows he has a captive audience, and he pauses dramatically, looking at each of them. "When this happens, Taquka-aq comes to the village in the night and shows her displeasure. Three times she has visited us these past two weeks, destroying fishing equipment and eating caches of fish. The elders are meeting tomorrow to decide how to appease her. The man will likely be asked to leave, and your father's portion of the catch going back to the village will be increased, so it can be given to Taquka-aq."

The excitement Sam was feeling changes to anxiety. Her dad explained to them how in exchange for the elders housing the fishermen in the village and allowing them port, they'd agreed on a certain percentage of their haul as payment. With that agreement now in dispute, she understands why he couldn't leave. The people of the village are obviously very friendly and Sam has no doubt her father will work it out, but even the possibility of the season being threatened is very concerning.

Tulock must pick up on Sam's unease, because he turns a smile towards her, before reaching out to set a comforting hand on her shoulder. "Your father is a wise man, Samantha, and all the elders respect him. This is not the first time that the Kodiaks have been displeased, and it will not be the last. We will reach a resolution, and celebrate our success together at the end of the season."

Before Sam has a chance to respond, the radio squawks, prompting Tulock to slip his headset back on and turn quickly to the controls. After a brief conversation, he once again hangs the headset on its peg and calls back to them over his shoulder. "We've got a nice tail wind and are making great time. Nothing but blue skies up ahead."

Since the conversation about Shadow Mountain appears to be over, Sam turns to look at Ally and John. While Ally's expression is a mix of concern and curiosity, John's is cautious.

"Sam … ," he draws going so far as to even point a finger at her. "Don't even *think* about it. We can't get involved in something this sensitive. Let your dad handle it."

"But, John," Cassy interjects swinging her legs out into the aisle to stretch them out. "Don't you think we could at least ask around?" she whispers, glancing towards the front of the plane. "Maybe listen to the whole legend and figure out what it was the guy was looking for that got him into trouble?"

"I'd love to hear an elder tell the whole story," John agrees. "But that's it. The other stuff isn't any of our business. If Sam and Hunter's dad wanted us to know, he would have told us." John speaks with determination, not caring who does or doesn't hear him.

"You're right," Kerry agrees. "I'm sorry that

I brought it up. My husband didn't imply that it was a big deal, though. I'm sure that Tulock is right and it'll be all smoothed over in no time."

"Seriously, guys," Hunter says. He's gone back to lounging in his seat. His feet, minus their shoes, are propped on either side of Cassy's head and she's doing her best to avoid them. Smiling at her unsuccessful attempt at evasion, he leans out to look at the other three kids. "Talking bears? I don't think this is anything that needs 'exploring'. Can we just enjoy a trip for once, without forcing some sort of life-altering adventure?"

Changing tactics, Cassy catches one of Hunters legs in the crook of her arm, and starts tickling his foot. The ensuing battle is a successful distraction, and the topics of vengeful bears and village disputes don't come back up during the next three hours of flight.

Once the novelty of flying in the floatplane wears off, they distract themselves with games, and watching Riley and Rocky's antics. The two are a funny pair, never seeming to tire of chasing each other up and down the length of the aisle. Eventually, it leads to both of them falling fast-asleep to the lulling hum of the plane.

Sam spends a good deal of time with her forehead pressed against the small window beside her. They're low enough that she can just make out the features of the landscape painted under them. It amazes her how vast the wilderness is, broken up only occasionally by small clusters of civilization. It's been a while since she saw such a development, and now a massive wall of mountains swell into view, reaching for the underbelly of the plane.

"Mr. Watchman," she calls while keeping her eyes firmly fixed on the scene taking form. "What in the world is that mountain range?"

"Call me Tulock," he gently reminds Sam as he turns to face her. "*That* is the beginning of the Alaska Boundary Range I told you about. It's part of the Coast Mountains, which form a ten-thousand-foot high north to south wall along the Alaskan border."

"Wow," Ally murmurs as she pushes her face to her own window. Cassy crowds onto Ally's seat with her and attempts to get a view, since her window faces the east and looks out over Canada, beyond the mountains.

40

"Look at all that water!" John exclaims, just as enthralled. "I didn't realize the ocean came inland so far here."

"That inlet marks the southernmost border of Alaska," Tulock explains. "You can now see how the first three hundred miles of Alaska is made up of more than a thousand islands, called the Alexander Archipelago."

"Hey, I remember studying about that last year!" Hunter states. Suddenly interested, he pulls at John until he moves and lets Hunter take his seat. "It was named after some Tsar dude in Russia. We had to color a map and it took *forever*. Cool!" he exclaims after getting a good look below them. "It actually kinda looks like the map!"

Sam shakes her head at her brother, but can't help smiling. She'll never understand how his brain works. She doesn't remember anything about Russian Tsar's, when it comes to Alaskan history, but she *does* remember the gold rush. "Was that area part of the whole gold thing?" she asks Tulock, stepping up to look out the front of the plane.

Tulock gestures to the co-pilot seat beside

him, and Sam eagerly sits in it. The view from up here is even more amazing, although the larger, panoramic windows have a dizzying effect on her. Gripping the armrests until her knuckles begin to turn white, Sam swallows hard and does her best to fight off the rising nausea.

Glancing sideways at her, Tulock raises his eyebrows. "You okay?"

Determined to hear him out, Sam nods her head vigorously and then instantly regrets it. Turning sideways in the seat, she tries to focus instead on the pilot. Based on his expression, she doesn't think she's doing a good job of convincing him that he isn't about to see what she had for breakfast.

"I'll be all right," Sam rushes to assure Tulock. "It's passing. What were you going to tell me about the gold?"

Hesitating, Tulock seems to come to a decision as he reaches into a compartment beside him and pulls out a bag. Handing it to Sam, he settles back in his seat. "The gold rush you're referring to started in the 1890s."

Sam absently studies the paper sack and then blushes when she realizes it's a vomit bag.

Holding onto it tightly, she turns a little more from the windows and listens intently.

"I wasn't born until the early 1960's, so I've only heard stories of it. But there wasn't much that happened in our area," Tulock explains. "The bulk of the explorers went to north of us by boat, up into the Klondike. We had some of the more adventurous pass by on foot, trying to pan along the way. That's not to say there isn't gold in our mountains. There is."

Sam leans forward with this revelation, her nausea forgotten.

"It's mostly found in the rivers, and has to be panned. To get anything significant is an arduous process, to say the least. The big gold is *inside* the mountains. It's called hard rock mining, where you go at the gold veins with a pick. At least, that's how it was done back then. Around our area the veins are too deep and the terrain too treacherous to make it worth the cost. So we were largely passed over during the rush."

"But people still pan for gold?" Hunter asks.

Sam looks over her shoulder to discover that her friends have all crowded forward to listen to the conversation. Smiling at the eagerness on her brother's face, she waits to hear Tulock's answer.

Shaking his head, the older man chuckles. "Son, people *always* pan for gold, but rarely find anything worth cashing in on. The river I mentioned is the closest in our region that's had any success. It doesn't even have what you would call an official name, but was dubbed 'rushing waters' by those that panned it in the 1970's. They set up an operation for years above the falls, deep in the Boundary Range. After the investors ran out of money, they abandoned it to the wilderness, and there it has rotted for the past forty years. Sorry," he adds, turning to look at his audience. "It's not much of a story. It's a beautiful area, though. Magnificent waterfalls and narrow ravines."

"It sounds incredible," Ally breathes.

Glancing at his watch, Tulock then taps at the controls and eventually scratches his jaw. "Well, we *have* made great time, thanks to that tail wind. We're about an hour out from Ketchikan. We could make the slight detour to the falls and still arrive on time."

"Really?" Cassy crowds up next to Sam and then pauses when she takes in the same view that challenged her friend's stomach. "I vote yes!"

Nodding in agreement, Sam voices her support of the plan, too.

"Well, unfortunately, this isn't a democracy," Tulock laughs. "Why don't you all take your seats and I'll determine if we can pull it off."

Sam is happy to return to her more limited window view, and the five of them fill Kerry in on the possible sightseeing. She's occupied with a fussing Riley, who wasn't happy when he woke from his short nap. The little boy has finally settled down now, but is still groggy.

After ten minutes, the plane suddenly takes a marked turn to the right, and begins to descend. Her stomach lurching again, Sam ignores it. "Are we going?" she asks Tulock while bouncing in her seat.

"I wasn't able to raise the base," their pilot explains. "But we're not expected in for another hour, so Marty's probably still at lunch. If the weather weren't perfect, I wouldn't do it, even though it's close by. But ..." it's obvious he's still questioning his decision. "We'll make it quick. It's a sight you won't soon forget!"

John works his way up the aisle, petting

Rocky as he steps over him. "Mind if I sit up here with you, sir?"

"Be my guest," Tulock replies. "Keep an eye out for a mountain peak shaped like an M. That'll be our landmark. The river is behind it."

Twenty minutes later, John lets out a whoop, and points ahead at something only he and Tulock can see. Sam once again pushes her face into the window as the plane descends even further, bringing the landscape into clearer focus. Rugged mountaintops reach up and they eventually come along even with them before dropping down in between.

"Oh my gosh!" Ally gasps, reaching over the seat to find Sam's hand.

Sam is too mesmerized to be afraid. A river takes shape under them and then disappears to plummet down the largest waterfall Sam has ever seen! The wilderness is raw in its beauty, a kaleidoscope of shades of green that define lush foliage clinging to the steep, rocky sides of the mountain.

"It doesn't look real!" Kerry exclaims. Riley climbs from his mother's arms and immediately begins to play with Rocky. She barely glances his way, since he's happy again, and the view is enthralling.

"I'll do one more lower pass over, and then we'll have to turn back!" Tulock calls out as the plane banks hard to swing back around.

Sam leans over to risk a look out the front windows just as a bizarre, gray flurry of motion erupts in front of the plane!

"Woah!" John yells. "What's tha -- "

Before he can finish, Tulock cuts him off with a shout of warning as there's a series of sickening thumps against the front of the plane. "Geese!" the pilot bellows.

Thumping turns into a knocking that sounds as if it's coming from inside the plane. "Everyone get your belts on!" Tulock orders, his voice betraying the fear enveloping them all.

As Sam fights to buckle her seatbelt with trembling hands, she realizes that the odd sounds have to be coming from the engines. The geese were sucked in! The plane begins to buck as the engines sputter. Horror-stricken, the scene playing out around her happens in slow motion.

John appears in the aisle, his face a pale mask of terror. He races down the length of the plane as it pitches wildly to the right, the engines now obviously losing power. Sam turns to watch him go and sees him scoop Riley up in his arms. The little boy and Rocky are at the back of the plane, oblivious to the danger.

Hunter reaches out to grab Rocky. As the two older boys buckle themselves in while holding their precious cargo, the floats skim the treetops.

The sound is like something torn from a movie, and Sam's eyes, wild with fear, seek out her best friend. She and Ally look at each other for what feels like an eternity, but then survival instinct takes over. Spinning back around, Sam bends forward and wraps her head in her arms. Her breath is rapid and muffled in her small cocoon of space, but it can't block out the sounds of the crash.

There's a moment of suspension as the plane bounces off the tree canopy and then plunges into open space, much like when a roller coaster crests a rise. Then, their world erupts into a series of screams and the sound of twisting metal.

5

AFTERMATH

"Sam! Sam, can you hear me?" John's voice edged with fear.

"Sam, *please* say something." Ally's voice muffled by loud sobs.

"Give her some room, you guys. Look – her eyes are fluttering. Her pulse is good, she'll be okay."

A woman's voice she can't quite place. How does she know her?

Sam forces her eyes open in an attempt to see who's speaking about her. The effort pays off with both a vision of a young woman leaning over her, as well as a headache. In an instant, the events leading up to her current situation come rushing back. Sam's assaulted by not only the memories of the crash, but the smell of burning rubber, the cries of Riley, and barking of Rocky.

Kerry. Riley's mom. Why is she talking like Ally's mom? Ally's mother is an intensive care nurse at their local hospital. Sam's been around her enough to recognize the take-charge demeanor that Kerry is now displaying. She's holding Sam's head in her lap, with a hand cupping each ear to hold her still. Her forehead feels like it was hit with a sledgehammer. Sam suspects she slammed it against the wall in front of her seat that divides the cockpit from the rest of the plane.

"I'm okay," Sam mumbles. It's supposed to come out sounding strong, but instead is almost lost amongst the other sounds.

"Sam!" Cassy cries. "She said something!"

Leaning over her while she speaks, Cassy comes into Sam's view. Her dark hair is a mess around her face, and tears streak through something that looks like jam smeared across her right cheek. Reaching out to touch her friend, Sam is horrified to realize it's blood. "Cassy! You're bleeding."

Laughing in relief, Cassy grabs on tight to Sam's outreached arm. "It's only a silly rug burn from the seat in front of me," she rushes to explain.

When she tries to sit up, Kerry's grip on her head tightens.

"Not so fast!" Kerry orders. "You took quite a hit, Sam. We need to make sure your neck isn't injured."

"Kerry is a nurse," Ally explains from where she's sitting at Sam's feet. Rocky is pushed up against her best friend's back, looking over her shoulder, and whining at Sam.

"I've worked in a family practice for the past two years, but I was an Emergency Medical Technician on an ambulance for three years before I got my nursing degree," Kelly says absently as she begins to prod at Sam's neck. "Does this hurt?"

Sam tries to shake her head but then remembers she isn't supposed to move. "No. Nothing hurts, really, except for my forehead."

Apparently not taking her word for it, Kerry continues her exam. "How about this? Does it hurt when I push here? Can you move your feet and hands for me? Good. Now, look into my eyes."

Sam looks up into Kerry's dark blue eyes. Removing a hand from Sam's neck, she holds it first over one eye, and then the other, checking to make sure her pupils expand and contract equally. Happy with what she sees, Kerry slips her hands down to Sam's back and helps her to slowly sit up.

"Do you feel nauseous? Any dizziness?"

Taking a moment to think about it, Sam closes her eyes and takes a deep, shuddering breath to steady herself. "No. None."

Now that Kerry's lap is empty, Riley is quick to scoot into it and she hugs her little boy tightly. Sam figures he was the first person she checked out after the crash, and he appears unharmed. "Thank goodness John had Riley in the backseat," Kerry breathes into her sons fair hair. "I braced myself against the wall instead of bending over like you, Sam, and I'm pretty sure both of my wrists are lightly sprained. I can't imagine if I'd had Riley on my lap!"

Finally able to look around, Sam notes that Hunter is crowded onto the seat behind her with Cassy, looking rather pale, but not obviously injured. John is standing in the opening to the cockpit, his attention split between their huddled group, and the pilot's seat.

Tulock!

"Is Tulock okay?" Sam demands while trying to stand up and realizes what an awkward position they're in on the floor.

"Let me go first," Kerry says decisively. "He said he was okay and that I should check on everyone else."

Sam sees small tendrils of smoke creeping along the ceiling as she watches Kerry stand, and a new wave of fear surges through her. "Something's burning!"

"It's the electrical equipment in the dash," John explains holding up a small fire extinguisher. "I already took care of it."

As Kerry steps over Sam and then around John, Ally leans forward to take hold of Sam's hands. First rising to their knees, they hug each other tightly.

"I was so scared," Ally whispers. "I couldn't wake you up."

Cassy wraps them both up in a big embrace. Without any space left, Hunter rests a hand gently on top of his sister's head. Looking up,

Sam gives him a smile and they share a rare moment without any jeers or teasing.

Turning, Sam is concerned to see that John has looked away from them to stare worriedly at whatever it is that Kerry is doing. While Tulock was able to talk right after the crash, that doesn't mean he isn't hurt. Breaking free of her friends, Sam staggers to her feet and then has to put a hand out to brace herself. The plane is tilted downward, casting the floor at an angle.

Rocky is instantly beside her, and she happily picks him up before stepping next to John. The smell of burning wires is stronger here, in the enclosed space. The large window she'd just been staring out is now shattered with a starburst pattern of cracks, obscuring the view of thick tree branches pressed up against it. The dashboard appears to be closer to the seats than before, as if the whole front of the plane is shoved in. She can see Tulock's legs wedged under the narrowed space, but his face is blocked by Kerry's back.

John puts a hand on Sam's shoulder, stopping her from going any further. "Wait," he says simply. "Give them room."

After a gut-wrenching ten minutes, Kerry

finally sighs and leans away from her patient. Tulock is exposed, his face contorted in pain, sweat beaded along his pallid forehead. Aside from some scratches on his cheek and hands, his upper body looks okay. His legs, however, are not.

"His left leg is broken," Kerry says matter-of-factly. "It's a compound fracture, which means that the bones are separated. I can't tell for sure, but I think one has broken through the skin."

"Don't the bones need to be put back in place as soon as possible?" John asks. When Kerry looks at him in surprise, he shrugs. "I've been a scout for years and I've had advanced wilderness survival training. I've never even seen a broken bone like that, though, so I've only read about it."

Nodding, Kerry smooths back the hair that's escaped from her pony. "Ideally, yes. The longer the bones are displaced, the worse the muscles contract and spasm around it, making it even more painful and harder to correct. The greatest concern, though, is infection. Which is why I really don't want to do *anything* with it out here other than bracing it. It's best to wait until we can get him to a hospital. How long do you think it'll be before someone gets here?" Kerry asks, turning back to Tulock. "More than a few hours?"

Sam didn't think it was possible for Tulock to look worse than he already does, but somehow his features darken even further. "That might be a problem," he says through clenched teeth. Looking from Kerry, to John, and then finally resting his steely gaze on Sam, the pilot breathes in a ragged breath. "No one knows where we are."

6

STRANDED

"What do you mean; no one knows where we are?" Ally cries. Stepping in closer to Sam, she grasps her friend's arms and does her best to look between her and John. She's dismayed at Tulock's condition, and panic begins to set in. "Don't you have one of those tracker things in here, so someone can find us?"

Shaking his head, Tulock gestures to the plane around him, the CB receiver still clutched in his right hand. "This is an old plane. It didn't come equipped with the type of technology you're referencing. There's a program here in Alaska to try to furnish all of us with an advanced satellite based GPS system. It's on our wish list, but is still extremely expensive. We use the most common form of GPS tracking for private planes, where our phone saves our location as we travel and then downloads the information at set points along the way. It isn't real-time and up here, isn't that often."

There's a long, silent pause as the realization of what Tulock is saying sets in.

"When was the last data download?" John is the first to ask.

Hesitating, Tulock tries to shift in his seat and the motion causes a groan of pain. "It was nearly an hour ago," he finally admits.

"But there's a flight plan, right?" Hunter asks. It's the first time Sam has heard him speak and his voice is hoarse. He and Cassy are standing close behind them with Riley.

"We're not on the flight plan, though," Sam reminds everyone. "And Tulock didn't get ahold of anyone to let them know we were coming out here. Right?"

Tulock agrees reluctantly. "The radio's busted," he adds, holding out the dead receiver. "Not even any static. I made the worst mistake a pilot can," he says quietly while tossing the useless equipment aside. "I got too comfortable.

Figured nothing could go wrong on such a nice day, and didn't follow my own rules. I should have never brought you up here without letting base know about the flight change. It's the wrong time of year for the geese to be congregating, too, or else I wouldn't have taken us down so low."

"But they'll come looking for us!" Cassy screams. "I mean, when we don't show up, they'll send out a search party." Growing desperate, Cassy struggles to pull her cell phone out of her back pocket with shaking hands. They all know there isn't any reception. Tulock told them a half hour ago that there wouldn't be until they were in Ketchikan.

"Yes! Yes, Cassy, they'll find us. Please don't panic. It's just going to take some time, and we'll have to take steps to make sure they see us," he adds, looking at the rest of them.

"How long?" Kerry asks.

"Our last known location will be recorded as about an hour south of where we deviated from our flight plan," Tulock explains. "Protocol will be to start the search there, in a widening and increasing pattern. However," he continues, wincing again as a new spasm of pain contorts his face momentarily, "the search will take them along the flight plan to our destination. When they don't find us, they'll expand the search, working back again in the opposite direction. We're Northeast of the flight plan by nearly fifty miles, but we should fall inside the secondary search."

"How long?" Kerry asks again.

"Six, maybe seven days. Possibly longer if the weather changes," Tulock discloses.

A week. Sam stops herself from gasping at the news, but Ally and Cassy don't try to hide their fear. Openly crying now, the two of them hug each other behind Sam. Steeling herself to their reality, Sam attempts to take in the bigger picture. They all have snacks with them and sleeping bags, and there's a river nearby. They'll be okay. However, looking at Kerry's expression, she isn't so sure about Tulock.

"We need to set your leg." Looking resolutely at Tulock, the young nurse doesn't try to sugarcoat anything. "And it's going to hurt."

Nodding, Tulock looks past Kerry to John. "First, you need to get the other kids off the plane. While I'm fairly certain you got the fire out, John, there's no certainty that it's safe in here. We can use it as a shelter if nothing flares up by tonight, but for now, we need to be cautious. There's a red first aid kit in with your bags, as well as emergency rations in a large black tote bag."

John immediately moves towards the exit, and everyone follows close behind. There's a moment of chaos when the door won't open at first, but with all of them pushing against it, they manage to scrape it open through the foliage.

The plane has come to rest up against several cedar trees, with the nose down in a small gulley up against a Cliffside. As Sam jumps down to the ground, she looks around in amazement. The trees are thick, and there's a clear path where the plane plowed through the branches. She has no idea how Tulock managed to keep the plane upright, let alone intact, and she suspects most other pilots wouldn't have managed so well.

The woods remind her of the rainforest back home, out on the Olympic Peninsula. Moss hangs down from the evergreens, and the ground is dense with underbrush and ferns. Although it's April, the air is crisp and it's a strong reminder that they *aren't* home. The newly broken cedar boughs and disrupted dirt and pine needles on the ground mix together to create a musty, heavy smell. A branch cracks nearby, and they all jump at the sound, unfamiliar with the animals in these mountains that could produce it.

When nothing further happens, they all breathe a collective sigh of relief and are motivated into action. Moving with purpose, they start pulling their belongings from the storage compartment, but the shock of the accident prevents them from saying much.

When a pile of luggage has formed behind the plane, John stands with is hands on his hips, looking around them in every direction. "I think it would be good to keep this rock formation to our backs," he suggests, pointing at the outcropping that the plane is nosed up against. "With the plane to our left, that only leaves the two other sides open, and we can build a large fire there. That way, we'll be well protected at night. I don't think any animals will wander into this area if we keep it built up."

Nodding in agreement, Kerry pulls the first aid kit aside and starts rummaging through it.

Pulling out an ace wrap, she holds it up. "Can someone wrap my wrist for me? I think my left one is fine, but my right one needs some support."

As Ally steps forward to help Kerry, Sam moves up next to John. While they can't see any distinct breaks in the trees around them, the sound of the rushing river is nearby. Beyond the plane, the mountains of the Alaskan Boundary tower above them, the rocky crags in stark contrast to the sky that almost has a purplish tinge. "So, Ketchikan is on the other side of those?" Sam asks, crossing her arms over her chest in a feeble attempt to fight off the chill in the air.

Staring down at her, John doesn't respond right away. He looks older than his sixteen years, and Sam notices a deep bruise forming over his left eyebrow. She's always thought him to be invincible, so the helplessness she sees in his vivid blue eyes is unsettling.

"It may as well be on another planet," he finally replies. "Planes have been known to go missing in these mountains and are never found."

"If you're trying to be reassuring, it isn't

working," Sam tries to tease, but the joke falls flat. It just isn't funny.

Glancing back at the rest of the group to make sure no one else is listening, John leans in closer. "At the least, we have to find a clearing where we can build a large signal fire."

"Three fires mean distress," Sam states.

John looks at her in surprise. "Right. And we'll need to collect things that will burn black. Maybe cut down the tires on the plane into small strips."

"I'm going to need your help, John."

Turning as one, Sam and John find Kerry standing behind them. She's slung the red backpack with the meager medical supplies over her shoulder. Riley is holding fast to her leg, with Rocky on his other side.

"Setting a compound fracture is way outside my scope of practice," she explains nervously. "I've seen it done by a physician several times, so I know how to do it, but the patient is usually sedated and given medication to make the muscles relax. Without any of that, it's going to take a lot of strength to pull the bone into place. My wrists are going to make it even more difficult."

"I can help, too," Hunter offers. "I'm small for my age, but I'm tougher than I look."

Happy to hear her brother sounding more like himself, Sam smiles at him. "Do you need sticks for a splint?"

"No," Kerry says. Reaching into the backpack, she pulls out a big roll of what looks like stiff foam. "This is called a SAM splint. It's a thin piece of metal coated with foam, so that you can bend it to whatever shape you need. It'll be perfect. I'll use the other two ace wraps in here to secure it. Unfortunately, there aren't any antibiotics, but there's a bottle of Ibuprofen."

"Here," John calls out to his sister. She turns just in time to catch the lighter he tosses at her. "You three collect as much wood as you can that's close by and get a fire started. First thing after we get Tulock squared away, we need to find some water, and we'll have to boil it."

"There's a bunch of bottled water in this bag," Hunter points out, unzipping the big black tote bag.

"We'll each need about four of those a day," John states.

They all do the simple math, and then look at each other remorsefully. They'll run out in less than two days.

"Right. So we find water," Hunter agrees.

Without any further discussion, the two boys follow Kerry back inside the plane. Sam, Cassy, and Ally distract themselves from the thought of what's happening to Tulock by gathering wood. Riley thinks it's a grand game, and sprints around the small clearing, proudly displaying each stick he picks up before throwing it for Rocky to fetch.

By the time the screams erupt from the cockpit, there's a modest pile of branches. Freezing, the three girls look at each other, eyes wide. Sam's headache spikes with the acceleration of her heart rate, reminding her that she has a head injury. Placing a hand to her forehead, she stumbles slightly before sitting down hard.

"Sam!" Ally shouts, quick to notice her friend's discomfort. "Do you need me to get Kerry?"

As Tulock's shouts fade into groans, Sam does her best to push the fuzziness aside. Rocky shoves his nose up under her chin and then firmly licks her across the throat, adding his concern. "I'm fine," she answers, laughing at her dog as he responds to her voice by curling into her lap. "Really. I think I just got a little scared. It made my head hurt more, but it's passing already."

"My head hurts, too," Cassy states sitting down next to Sam. Prodding gingerly at her scraped cheek, she glances sideways at the plane. There's no longer any sounds coming from within.

Ally stares at her two best friends. Their normally cheerful faces are instead full of fear and dismay, their hair a mess, and dried blood smudged in various spots. Looking up at the vast wilderness surrounding them, the sudden thought of her parent's crashes through Ally's state of shock, and a loud sob escapes her. "Our parents are going to be terrified!" she wails her hands flying to her face. "Oh my gosh! They're going to think we're all *dead*!"

As Ally's words slam home, Sam's head pounds again. Reaching out blindly for her friend as tears blur her vision, she pulls Ally down to join her and Cassy. She's right; their parent's *will* fear the worst. But she knows that they won't give up hope and will keep searching until the crash site is found. The feeling of hopelessness is horrifying and Sam has never been so scared in all her life.

"They know that so long as we're together," Cassy urges, pulling them all in for another group hug, "that we'll be okay."

Nodding, Ally wipes at her nose. "I just feel so bad for mom. How will she stand it?" Another fresh round of tears stream down her face, and her spattering of freckles become camouflaged under the mud they create.

"Our parent's will be together, just like us," Sam reassures her hiccuping around her own ragged breaths.

The three girls sit that way for several minutes, arms wrapped tight around each other's shoulders. Eventually, their tears dry and they're forced to face the situation that they're in.

"We should start the fire," Sam urges. "It's actually pretty cold out here, even though the sun is shining. We don't want Tulock to be cold."

Ally stands first, and then helps both Sam and Cassy to their feet. The three of them are thankful for something to do and work together to get the fire roaring to life. By the time John and Hunter carry Tulock out on a sleeping bag, the heat is seeping outward.

Kerry scoops up Riley and watches anxiously as the boys gingerly lower him to the ground. "I think I got the bone set okay, and the circulation to his foot seems good. But … there's still a risk of a serious infection."

"It takes more than a broken leg to keep me down," Tulock jokes. When Sam looks at him with surprise, he chuckles. "I won't lie, that hurt like the dickens, but it actually feels better than it did before, now that everything is back where it should be."

John squats down next to Tulock and points up at the mountains. "How far would say that range is?"

His smile fading, Tulock cocks his head sideways. "Do you mean by plane?"

"No," John answers. "By trail."

After a long pause, Tulock slowly shakes his head. "It's at least a good forty miles, over dangerous terrain. It's absolutely out of the question," he adds. "No one is hiking to that mountain."

"But that lower peak in between the others is the perfect place to light a signal fire," John pushes.

"*That* is Shadow Mountain," Tulock explains with a faraway look in his eyes. "And the home of Taquka-aq."

7

BEN SHADOW

"The same Shadow Mountain that you told us about, where trespassers are like, eaten by *bears*?" Hunter asks Tulock, looking to John for emphasis.

"There have been several attacks over the years," Tulock confirms, still staring out at the mountain. "The most infamous involved a man named Ben Shadow."

Crinkling her nose in thought, Sam glances up at the peak in question. "Was it named after him?"

"No. It was named long ago due to how it falls within the shadows of the other mountains." Tulock pauses to take a drink of water and wipe at the sweat still dampening his forehead. "Ben

Shadow was a young man on an adventure. It was the mid 1950's, and he was traveling on foot to the gold-rich grounds to the north. He was following in the footsteps of his grandfather, who was part of the Klondike gold rush. When he stopped in our village to rest, he fell in love with both my great-aunt, Auka, *and* the mountain.

"He was fearless of Taquka-aq, and spent days at a time exploring the land that no one else dared travel. Ben believed in fate, and he felt that the mountain was his namesake. When the elders had enough they gathered with him, and it was then that Ben Shadow claimed that Taquka-aq spoke to him in her human form, giving him permission to mine for gold. Of course, most everyone was skeptical. But as the months went by, opinions changed. Ben built a small cabin on the far side of the mountain and started bringing in samples of gold to have tested. He remained unharmed and the village wasn't punished.

"I was not born yet, but my great aunt Auka told me the whole story once, filling in the details that the legend leaves out. She begged him to leave the gold and stay in the village with her, but he was determined to make his claim and build her a proper home. When the samples kept testing poorly, he came down to the village less often, and the quest for gold changed him as it does most men.

"Two years after Ben Shadow first arrived, the shredded remains of his winter coat was found by other miners looking for his claim. The claw of a giant Kodiak bear was left embedded in the leather. Ever since, the wrath of Taquka-aq is leveraged more easily against those who trespass, and many believe that Ben Shadow took the same form and joined her on the mountain to keep those from what he believes was always his."

There's a long, drawn-out silence and the fire crackles and pops in the absence of any conversation. Although it's only late afternoon, shadows have begun to gather under the thick canopy of trees, concealing whatever secrets the forest protects.

"Ummm ... yeah," Ally stutters. "I vote with Tulock. We should stay here and work on building a signal fire nearby."

"I second that," Hunter offers.

"If you all remember, we already established that while under my care, this is not a democracy," Tulock chuckles. "You *will* stay here." Pointing at the provisions that are stacked into a pile, his voice gathers strength. "It looks like we'll have enough to eat for a week, but you need to take it and store it in the metal container in the cargo hold of the plane. My understanding of the area is that the bears aren't as thick out here on this side of the river, but it's still a higher concentration than nearly anywhere else in the world. They have a freakish nose for food, so it is of the utmost importance to *never* leave anything out, other than water."

He doesn't need to say it twice. The kids busy themselves with following his orders, storing the food, as well as gathering more firewood. Next, Tulock has them line up their backpacks and tote bags, as well as the emergency gear that was on the plane.

Nodding in approval at the additional survival gear John takes from his trek pack, Tulock points to his fire making implements. "We shouldn't be needing that, but it's good you have it. How about bear spray?"

Sam steps forward with a large can grasped in her right hand. "My dad said we had to bring some," she explains. "Both Hunter and I have a can. We already had it with our camping gear in the garage."

"We've only got one," John adds. "I always carry one with me on hikes, but Ally and Cassy didn't have a chance to get any before we left."

"Those will do," Tulock states. "I have two more in with the emergency supplies. We should always keep at least one here by the fire. No one leaves this space without a minimum of two people and two canisters of spray. Understood?"

Everyone quickly agrees, and John pulls one of the cans from the black tote bag and places it just beyond the heat of the fire. For whatever reason, the discussion confirms the seriousness of the situation, and the mood around the fire is somber.

"Should we go look for water now, before it gets dark?" Kerry asks. She's sitting next to Tulock, a sleepy Riley in her lap.

"Yes. John, you and two others go find the river. It's obviously close by so simply follow the sound. The problem will be locating a safe spot to access it. As you saw from above, the river here has carved out a ravine. Most likely, the trees will take you right to the edge, so be cautious. Do you have a compass?" When both John and Sam pull one out of their bags, Tulock smiles. "Good. Make note of the direction, and turn to the south with you come to the water. Follow it downstream. If you don't find a spot within a mile or so, come back and try again tomorrow. It will be dark shortly after seven."

"We'll look for a clearing for the signal fire along the way," John adds, pulling a collapsible plastic jug from Tulock's bag. It's meant for gathering drinking water, and with it are a tin cooking pot and other utensils.

Sam and Ally volunteer to go with John, and soon the three are deep into the woods, the safety of the fire left behind. The ferns and stinging nettles make the trek slower than they would like, but it doesn't take long to reach the edge of the ravine. It's a good twenty feet down to the river, and when they don't find a safe path to it, they do as Tulock directed and follow it downstream.

John leads the way, with Ally in the middle and Sam bringing up the rear. Clutching her bear spray tightly, she keeps looking back over shoulder, sure that a bear is sneaking up on her. As she peers into the dense foliage, it dawns on her how difficult it'll be for a plane passing overhead to spot them. The trees *do* lead right up to the edge, sometimes growing out over it, the roots clawing at the side of the cliff.

"John," Sam calls out, her voice sounding extra loud since none of them has spoken for several minutes. "How is a rescue plane going to see us? I haven't seen a clearing anywhere yet that's bigger than the small one back at camp. And that's only because the plane knocked a couple of trees down."

"They aren't going to see us," John answers. "At least, not the way things are now. The smoke from our fire might be seen during the day, but nothing will show through at night. There's an ax in with all that gear. When we get back, I'll work on clearing out some of the smaller saplings and trees around our spot. I think our best bet is to make the area around the crash site as visible as possible, and set up the signal fires right there. But what we *really* need to do, is get to the top of Shadow Mountain. The search plane should be passing not too far south of there in a couple of days. If we can get three good fires going before then, they're bound to see it!"

"But Tulock isn't going to let us," Ally counters. "You heard him. It's too dangerous."

"And the search party will be passing back over us on their way back," Sam adds. "We should be able to get some really good fires set up by then. Why do you think it's so important to be found sooner?" Sam knows John well enough to realize something's up. Of all of her friends, he is usually the most cautious and levelheaded.

Stopping, John looks back at his sister and Sam, his handsome face clouded with concern. "Because Tulock might not have that long."

8

DESPERATE MEASURES

The next morning is Monday, and it's doesn't start well.

Huddled together around the roaring fire, the six figures hold their hands out towards the warming flames. It was a cold night. Although the plane offers a lot of protection, it's too big inside to retain much heat, and with the front window broken, the cold air has a way inside. As soon as the sun started to filter through the trees, John and Kerry were outside piling wood on.

Tulock is sick. Laying a safe distance from the fire, he's wrapped in the sleeping bag he was carried back out on. Shivering, he moaned when he was first set on the ground but has now slipped into a restless sleep.

Kerry's mood noticeably darkened after examining his leg. Riley and Rocky are still asleep on the plane snuggling, and she glances over at the open doorway occasionally. Wringing her hands, she finally clears her throat and gestures at the kids to gather closer to her. "His leg is infected."

The declaration is straightforward but it still takes a moment for the implication behind it to sink in. Sam's stomach tightens and she's surprised to discover that it's possible to be more anxious than she already was. "That can be really serious, right?" she asks, searching Kerry's face for answers.

When the nurse doesn't respond right away, John speaks up. "You should tell them what you told Hunter and me yesterday," he urges. "After you set his leg."

"Well, yeah," she breathes heavily. "This is exactly what I was afraid of. I'm pretty sure the bone is back in place and circulation to his foot is good. There isn't any major bleeding. However, the bone was exposed long enough to have a very high risk of infection. If he were at the hospital, he would have been given IV antibiotics to start with, and then a good month worth of oral. I knew he had a good chance of developing something, but I was really hoping it wouldn't show up for a few days. But it's already festering, meaning there's an unhealthy discharge from the wound, and he's definitely got a fever, which is a sign that his body is fighting an infection."

Shuddering, Ally leans into Sam and takes hold of her arm. "What can we do?"

Shaking her head, Kerry throws another log on the fire, sending up sparks. The flash of light causes deeper shadows to dance across her face, making her next words even more ominous. "Nothing. I can try to control the fever with the Ibuprofen, and clean the wound several times a day, but it's the infection we can't see that's dangerous. Once it hits the bloodstream, he can develop sepsis, which is a life-threatening condition."

"How many days?"

Everyone turns to look at Sam. Her voice is steady, but her eyes glisten with tears.

"How many days until his life is in danger?" she presses.

"Every person's immune system is different,"

Kerry answers. "It's possible to have a localized infection for quite some time before it spreads, but his fever concerns me. That, along with the condition of the wound indicates that it's rapidly progressing. He likely needs advanced care in two to three days, or else -- " Unable to finish, Kerry looks down at her hands.

"But Tulock said the search party won't be out this way for at least *six*!" Cassy cries. Stepping forward, she grabs onto Sam's other arm. "We have to *do* something!"

"Come on," John orders as he steps away from the reach of the fire and towards the brightening woods. "We have a lot of work to do."

"I don't like the sound of that," Hunter replies but is already following his friend.

"We'll have to stack enough firewood for a week, clear out these small trees nearby, and set up the signal fires. Then, we'll hang blankets across the entrance to the cockpit of the plane so that it stays warmer in there at night. Oh, and we'll need to get as much water collected and boiled as we can."

"And why the urgency to do all of that?"

Kerry questions, hands on her hips.

"Because," John replies while pointing up at Shadow Mountain, "The only hope of rescue in the next two days is at the top of that mountain, and I'm going to get there."

***

"I'm going with you," Hunter says without hesitation.

Sam is surprised at how quickly her brother jumps on board with the idea. She, on the other hand, was expecting this. "All five of us should go."

Ally and Cassy look at Sam nervously, but don't object. They've been through so much together, that the thought of being separated is more upsetting than a hike through the woods.

"Uh-uh, no way," Kerry says adamantly. "I could get onboard with John and Hunter going. These are extreme circumstances, and I know that we need to do something about it. I can't go. I need to stay here with Tulock, and Riley is way too little for something like that, especially with my sprained wrists. But, Sam, you're twelve years old. I'm not about to let you traipse off into the wilderness!"

Her face burning with humiliation, Sam stops herself from blurting out a defensive remark. She knows that Kerry has a valid point. Except that Kerry doesn't know her. Swallowing first, Sam does her best to sound reasonable. "You're right. I turn thirteen next month. But I've done a ton of hiking, Kerry, and one thing my dad always says is that there's safety in numbers. Is there really that much of a difference if I'm lost in the mountains here with you, or out there with John and the others?"

Riley chooses this time to emerge from the plane, crying for his mom. Sam is thankful for the distraction, and kneels down to pet Rocky as he darts over to her.

"You're right about numbers," John agrees, surprising Sam. "When we get to any steep terrain, it'll be better if we can tie off with two or three to a rope. Bears are also less likely to charge us if they hear a larger group. But we don't *all* need to go. Kerry might need help."

Sam was beginning to get defensive again,

but John's remark stops her. Feeling ashamed for not thinking of the young woman, she turns back to Kerry. "I'm sorry," she says. "We can't all go and leave you here alone! I'll stay with you."

Laughing, Kerry straightens from where she got Riley settled next to Tulock. "I appreciate your concern, Sam, but John isn't the only one here with wilderness survival training. I've been a volunteer with our local search and rescue for years. I've even done a lot of solo hiking and camping, so that has nothing to do with my reluctance to let you go. I'd be just fine. Especially with the plane to keep us all safe at night.

"Listen," she continues, crossing her arms over her chest. "Maybe I've been underestimating you all. Let's be honest. Our plane crashed. We're in the middle of nowhere without any means of communication and no one knows where we are. We're a week away from a likely rescue, with a man who may very well have much less time than that. John is right. Our best hope right now is to get the three signal fires lit on the top of that mountain." Pointing out at the peaks for emphasis, she steps closer and lowers her voice.

"At this point, I don't care how you do it. Maybe it *is* best if you all stick together, or the girls can stay here with me. Either way, you need to leave as soon as possible."

"That dog is going to be your best bear alarm you could have."

Startled by the gravelly voice, Sam turns to see that Tulock has woken up, and is propped up on his elbows. His face is red and feverish, his eyes glassy. Looking down at Rocky, Sam isn't quite sure what he means.

"If you all insist on this rebellion, then you should at least listen to my advice. Dogs have a sixth sense for bears. Rocky there will alert you when one is getting close, and might even succeed in holding one off for a bit. Their bark confuses them, at least momentarily."

Sam pulls Rocky close. The thought of being separated from him is even more upsetting than being left out of the rescue attempt.

"Well, we can' take Rocky and not Sam," Hunter states. "That dog would be so busy whining for her, that he would never hear the bear!"

Sam has to restrain herself from launching

herself at her brother and wrapping him up in a big hug. The unlikely support is a precarious thing, and she's afraid he might take it back.

"It's decided, then," Tulock agrees. "You'd all better go about your tasks, then. You've got at least twenty hours of hiking ahead of you and the morning will be gone soon."

Sam continues to stare at Tulock for a minute, and then looks at Kerry. When the woman nods in agreement with the plan, Sam isn't sure whether to be relieved or scared.

9

RUSHING WATERS

"What if we can't find a safe place to cross?" Ally stops when her brother doesn't answer the question. "John!" she shouts. "What will we do?"

The five friends are spread out single-file, with John in the lead and Sam at the back with Rocky. They've been following the river for nearly an hour, without any sign of it widening and slowing down.

It took them several hours to complete all the tasks around the makeshift camp before they left. Sam dodged another bullet when Kerry demanded she evaluate her again before allowing her to go. The Ibuprofen made the headache go away, and it hasn't come back again. Aside from feeling a little sluggish, like she overslept, Sam isn't suffering from any other effects of a possible concussion. Kerry told her that if she'd thrown up, was dizzy, or confused, she would be concerned. The fact that the headache went away indicates that she only got a good bump to her head, and anything more dangerous would have shown up by now.

Stopping alongside Ally, Sam squints up at the sun. Thankfully, it's another clear day, but she's still grateful for the sweatshirt she's wearing. It can't be more than fifty degrees out. Shifting her stuffed backpack, she studies Ally's face. Her friend doesn't usually talk to John that way. They're all way past their comfort zones and definitely on edge.

"What do you want me to say?" John demands. Spreading his arms out towards the river, he then throws them up in the air. "I can't control this. Tulock said it was a good five miles before this widens and slows down. I'm guessing we've gone three so far. We'll get across, Ally," he ads in a calmer voice. "It really doesn't matter if he's wrong, and we end up going *ten* miles. Just keep an eye on Shadow Mountain," he suggests

while pointing to their goal in the distance.
"We're still a long ways off from being even with
it."

"It's called Rushing Waters for a good
reason," Hunter observes. Standing looking
down over the edge of the ravine, he tosses a
rock into the whitewater.

"Tulock wouldn't have told us we can cross it
if it were too dangerous," Cassy states, stepping
up to throw her own rock. "When this ravine
widens and the water gets shallow, the current
should let up, too." When Hunter turns to look
at her quizzically, she smiles. "One of our
summer field trips last year with the afterschool
program, was to go white water rafting. Our
guide explained how the water ran during our
orientation, and I guess it stuck with me."

Sam vaguely listens to the conversation. She's
come to the conclusion that the reason Tulock
suddenly changed his mind about this rescue
attempt, wasn't so much about self-preservation,
as it was to get them out of the campground. If
there was really a chance that he could die in the
next few days, he doesn't want them around to
see it. Gritting her teeth, she re-positions her

heavy pack and calls out to everyone. "We're wasting time, you guys. Let's go!"

They *will* get to Shadow Mountain in time.

***

"I don't understand why we can't just tie it around my waist." Ally is standing in ankle-deep water. Her shoes are tied together by their laces and draped around her neck to keep dry. Holding the nylon rope in her hands, she's looking out fearfully at the wide expanse of water.

"Because, if you fall and don't get back up on your feet right away," John explains patiently, "the rope will act like an anchor and hold you under the water. The same way it does if you fall when you're waterskiing and don't let go."

"Just don't let go of the rope," Sam says. Hugging Ally awkwardly while balancing barefoot on the rocks, she fights down her own wave of fear. Sam isn't scared of the water. Both she and Ally are excellent swimmers. But this water is numbingly cold, and although it doesn't look any deeper than a couple of feet, it's still moving quite fast.

Ally and Cassy don't have any extra weight since Sam, John, and Hunter are the only ones with backpacks. They decided to leave the awkward tote bags behind, and split all of their supplies up between the three packs before they left.

John's several feet ahead of them in the river with a long stick to test the water depth, followed by Cassy, Ally, Sam, and then Hunter as the anchor. Hunter *does* have the rope tied around him, both because he's the anchor and to keep his arms free so he can carry Rocky.

"Can we stop talking and just do this?" Hunter urges. "We've only walked about seven miles so far, and although this water feels good on my feet, they're getting numb really fast. We have a long ways to go still today, so I think we should get out of here as fast as possible."

For once, Sam agrees with her brother, and gently nudges Ally from behind. Soon, the slack in the rope between them is taken up and they're spread out across the river. John makes it past the middle without it going above his thighs.

"It's not that bad!" he shouts. "But watch where you step. There are some big rocks out here!"

John's about ten feet from the shore when Cassy reaches the deepest spot. Since she's several inches shorter than he is, it swirls around her hips, tugging relentlessly. Holding tightly to the rope, she slides her feet cautiously along the slick rocks, searching for the next safe spot to step. Breathing a sigh of relief, she finds a tall boulder under her and is able to step up and out of the worst of the current.

Ally isn't so lucky.

"Sam!" Ally cries out desperately.

Sam looks up just in time to see Ally slip sideways off the same rock Cassy was on moments before. The ground must slope away alongside it, because she's plunged into water up to her chest and the cold water robs the scream from her throat as she's pulled under.

Struggling to reach her best friend, Sam watches in terror as the force of the water rips the rope from Ally's hand. Not giving any thought to her own safety, Sam acts instinctively. She's vaguely aware of Cassy calling out to John as she unsnaps the straps of her backpack and shrugs it off. Throwing it back towards Hunter, her vision is narrowed as she dives headfirst downstream.

10

THE WILDS OF ALASKA

The cold, swift water swirls over Sam's head and the current threatens to push her down into the rocks. Fighting to break the surface, she immediately rolls over onto her back and points her feet downstream, a technique she was taut while whitewater rafting with her family two summers ago.

In spite of her precautions, Sam is immediately slammed in the shoulder blade by a passing boulder, and she knows she's in trouble. Aware of splashing and yells upstream from the rest of the group, she scans the water nearby and spots Ally's red hair.

"Ally!" Sam tries to call, but water pours in her mouth and it comes out as a gurgle instead.

Pale arms flail near the mess of red hair. Sam ditches her safety approach and flips back onto her stomach, sticking her feet down to try and find purchase. Instead, she ends up stubbing both of her big toes on passing rocks, but still manages to push off towards Ally. With long, broad strokes, Sam reaches her as they rush towards a huge cedar tree that's fallen into the water.

"Strainer!" John hollers. "Sam, a strainer!"

Fighting to keep her head above the whitewater, the words don't mean anything to Sam. But as they get closer to the cedar, she can see several large branches that are half-submerged. Suddenly, she recalls the discussion about strainers one bright, summer day during a water-safety class. They get their name by the straining effect that takes place as the rushing water passes through the tree. They're deadly to a swimmer. If she and Ally are caught up in the force of it, they'll be pinned underwater among the branches, too big to pass through to the other side.

"Sam!" Ally gasps. They were both in the same class.

Both girls thrash in the water, trying desperately to reach the safety of the shore while avoiding the hazardous rocks. It's clear that Ally is tiring, and Sam manages to hook her left arm through Ally's left.

"Hold on!" Sam demands while looking back upstream.

Hunter and Cassy have reached the shore and John is running recklessly downstream, Rocky barking furiously at his heals. John is clutching a large stick. As Sam watches, he passes them, and then splashes into the water, just before the lethal strainer.

"Grab it, Sam!" he yells.

With all the strength she has left, Sam hauls Ally with her towards the lifeline. Her feet touch bottom and stay. "Stand up, Ally!" Looking at her best friend, she imagines that her own eyes are just as wild. "Stand up!" she says more forcefully. "It's not that deep."

Shaking off her paralyzing terror, Ally forces her numb legs to obey and is relieved to discover that Sam is right. It's shallow enough that they can resist the force of the water and stay on their feet. But it's still waist-deep, and she can't hardly feel the lower half of her body or her hands. John is about ten feet away from them and moving closer, the stick almost within reach.

Huddling together, Sam and Ally shiver in the icy water, slowly moving towards safety. Inches away, Ally slips. Letting out a yelp, she tightens her grip on Sam and as they both start to go down, Sam wraps her right hand around the stick.

"Hold on!" John calls while looking to his right at the nearby strainer. Backing up, he pulls both of the girls through the swirling current.

Her mind is surprisingly clear as Sam focuses on her hand. She can't let go. That's her only thought as she then looks up at John. When she sees his ice-blue eyes relax and then move towards them, she realizes that they're safe.

***

The cracking of the fire is a reassuring sound, but Sam doesn't think she'll ever be warm enough. Holding her hands out towards the welcoming heat, she snuggles closer to Rocky in her lap, thankful that she can at least feel her fingers again.

"Well, that could have gone better," Hunter jeers. Walking up with another armload of wood, he tosses a big chunk on the hastily made bonfire.

"We made it across and we're all safe," John counters.

"I don't …. have any … clothes left," Ally murmurs through clattering teeth.

In addition to the survival gear, food, and water, they each brought one change of clothing with them.

"We should have taken our pants off before we crossed," John states. They've all changed into their dry clothes and he's busy wringing out their wet garments before laying them out on the rocks in front of the fire. "That was a stupid mistake. I don't even know if we should bother packing this stuff back up. It isn't going to dry enough to wear again, and it'll weigh us down."

Sam eyes her favorite pairs of jeans and silently decides it'll be worth the hassle. At least they had enough sense to take off their sweatshirts and shoes. Thankfully, Hunter caught the backpack she threw at him, so everything else is dry. Well, except for Ally's shoes. Good thing they didn't float away. Putting an arm around Ally, she rubs her back vigorously. "It's okay. We don't have any more rivers to cross, and we really shouldn't need any other clothes. We won't be out here long enough. Right, John?"

Nodding, John starts re-packing his bag. "If we can make it halfway tonight, and then reach the summit by tomorrow night, we can have the signal fires ready to go in the morning."

"I thought the whole point to the fires was that they're visible at night," Cassy counters. She faired the best out of the group in the river crossing, and didn't even bother changing her pants. They're made for hiking and dry quickly.

"The search planes won't be out at night," John explains. "Tulock said it's too dangerous. They'll be looking in the daylight for any wreckage, and smoke. That's why we want to make them as visible as possible. I brought a few strips of cut rubber from the tires, and once the fires are hot enough, we can throw some green wood on them, too."

"Are you warm enough, Ally?" Sam questions noticing that her friends' shivering has finally stopped.

"We really need to get moving," John adds looking at the sun that has already started to slip down the far side of the sky. "It's got to be getting close to three already."

"I'm okay," Ally says bravely. "I honestly think you got the worst of it, Sam. Look at all of the bruises on your arms! Are you sure you didn't hit your head? Kerry said it's really important that you don't hurt it again for several weeks."

"I'm fine," Sam replies, waving her off. Getting slowly to her feet, she pulls Ally up next to her before testing her legs out. Contrary to what she said, pretty much everything hurts. Except her head. Luckily, that was the one part of her body she kept off the rocks. Rolling her shoulders, she winces and remembers the first hit on her shoulder blade. *That will make the backpack more of a challenge*, she thinks to herself.

In a short amount of time, they have the fire extinguished and leave the rocky beach of the river behind for the lush rainforest. It's like stepping into a different world.

Before crossing the river, they had hugged the edge of the ravine so that they didn't have to deal with the dense underbrush. Once that levelled out, they'd simply followed the rocky shore until it got shallow enough to cross.

Now, the temperate rainforest wraps around them. It's a damp, green world of old growth Cedars, Sitka Spruce, and Western Hemlock. The floor of the woods is a blanket of spongy moss, ferns, and clusters of Devil's Claws. The odd plant is familiar to the group from Western Washington, where it's also native. What looks like a lone branch sticking up from the ground, sometimes six feet tall or more, it's covered in spikes and topped with a halo of green leafs and a delicate flower. The spikes are extremely painful, and dangerous to anyone that's allergic to the toxin in it.

"This is crazy!" Cassy says after hiking in silence for nearly an hour. Slipping a second time on the side of a fallen cedar she's trying to climb over, she smiles at Sam as she helps give her a boost. "This will take forever if it's like this the whole way."

"I'm sure it'll thin out the higher we get," John replies. "At least, I hope it does. Otherwise, you're right. We might not make it in time."

"See any bear poop?" Hunter asks. "I mean, shouldn't we be looking for it? I can see how a bear could get really close without you even knowing," he adds while watching the trees.

Sam lifts Rocky over the tree and then Hunter joins everyone else on the other side. She can tell that John is eager to press on, but she takes a moment to make sure the bear spray is firmly attached to the belt loop of her pants. Hunter and John also have a bottle. They left the other two at the camp with Kerry and Tulock.

"Rocky doesn't seem alarmed." Sam tries to sound reassuring, but her stomach is in knots. They don't even know if the poodle really has a natural instinct for bears or not.

"Well, then you take the back for a while," Hunter whines. "I need a break from looking over my shoulder."

Agreeing with a shrug of her shoulders, Sam and Rocky fall in last when John starts out again. She quickly understands her brother's complaint. The forest is alive with unfamiliar sounds and moving shadows. Having your back exposed makes it all feel threatening. Jumping at every cracking branch, Sam is soon carrying the bear spray in her hand, at the ready.

Almost two hours later, the amount of fallen trees finally starts to diminish, and the canopy thins out to let in more sunlight. Sam notices less ferns and moss, and more grasses. The trade off to the more easily traveled terrain is that it's also becoming steeper. The burn in her thighs is turning into a deep ache, and she's fallen behind. Barely able to see the bright red of Hunter's backpack anymore, she's about to call out and demand a break, when Rocky begins to bark.

Spinning around, Sam brings up the can, half-expecting to see a giant Kodiak bear crashing towards her. Instead, she's met with an eerie silence in the wake of the barking that feels almost tangible. There's a stillness in the trees that wasn't there before. Leaning down, she reaches blindly to pet the top of Rocky's head and discovers that he's quivering. The hairs on the back of her neck slowly rise, and with it, the intense feeling that she's being watched.

11

SHADOW MOUNTAIN

"Sam?" Ally whispers her friend's name. She turned back to check on her when she noticed Sam was lagging behind. Frozen, her head is tilted as Sam listens for something. But the woods are eerily quiet.

Jumping at the sound of Ally's voice, Sam starts to turn towards her, almost missing the subtle movement off to the left. Spinning back to face it, she peers into the shadows, trying to discern if there's anything solid hidden there.

A low rumble starts to build in Rocky's throat, and Sam looks down, surprised. She's never heard him growl this way. The hair at the nape of his neck is standing on end, reminding Sam of her own reaction moments before.

"Let's get out of here," Ally begs. Grabbing at Sam's arm, she tugs. "Maybe it's a bear!"

"No," Sam disagrees. "Bears don't *hide*, Ally." Still watching the trees, she allows Ally to pull her backwards and thankfully, Rocky follows.

"If you don't think it's a bear," Ally counters, helping direct Sam over another fallen log, "then why are you holding up the bear spray?"

Looking down at the death grip she has on the can, Sam laughs at herself. "I guess I figure it'll work on pretty much anything that has eyes," she explains. Clipping it back to her belt loop, she finally turns away and begins climbing at a faster pace.

"What do you think that was?" Ally questions after the two have caught back up to the other kids.

"Did you see it?" Sam asks hopefully. She still isn't sure if she didn't just imagine it.

"See what?" Ally's face has gone a shade paler.

"Nothing," Sam mumbles, disappointed. "It was probably nothing. It's spooky out here. It's hard to even see anything through all the underbrush. I'm glad it's finally thinning out."

"Well, *Rocky* definitely thought something was there!" Ally states. She knows Sam is trying to make light of it for her sake, and she doesn't like to be babied. "Now isn't the time to brush stuff off, Sam. If there's some sort of animal stalking us, we need to know!"

"Need to know what?"

Sam turns from the lecture Ally is giving her, to roll her eyes at her brother. *Great,* she moans inwardly. *Now I'll be teased endlessly about this!*

"Rocky was growling at something in the woods," Ally quickly interjects.

Sam looks at her best friend approvingly. She knows that Ally is right and she needs to tell the others what she thought she saw, but starting with Rocky's reaction helps make it more believable.

"Did you see anything?" Hunter is reaching for his bear spray as he says it, his expression instantly turning serious.

"Maybe," Sam offers. "I can't be sure if it was just a trick of the shadows, but it was the same area that Rocky was pointing at."

"How big was it?" Cassy asks coming to stand next to Hunter. "What did it look like?"

John remains silent, crossing his arms over his chest as he waits for Sam to answer. Looking down from his gaze, she kicks at a loose rock.

"It almost looked like … a man."

"Well, why didn't you call out?" Hunter demands. "Maybe he can help us! Maybe he's part of a search party!"

Sam puts a hand out to stop her brother, who's actually starting to move back down the mountain. "No!" she shouts. "It wasn't like that." Struggling to find the right words, she frowns in frustration. "It was more of a shadow, like a shape. It was looking out from *behind* a tree and as soon as I turned towards it, it disappeared. That's when Rocky started growling." Looking around at her captive audience, Sam decides she doesn't care if she gets teased. "Whatever it was, didn't want to be seen."

"Here we go!" Hunter declares throwing his hands up in the air. "A plane crash wasn't dramatic enough for you, Sam? You need to throw in some mystical creature or ghost, too?"

"Take it easy," John cautions his friend. "It was probably an animal, but if Rocky reacted too, I'll bet Sam is right. There's something out there, so we need to be extra cautious. I don't think a bear would be tracking us, but a mountain lion certainly could. We already know the wildlife is dangerous, so no more spreading out like that," he adds looking again at Sam. "Safety in numbers. Remember?"

Nodding silently, Sam resists the urge to get into an argument with her brother. Hunter thrives on it, and she knows it wouldn't accomplish anything. "Let's just keep moving," she finally says. "But maybe not so fast. My legs are killing me!"

"Mine are, too," Cassy agrees. "How much further do we need to go today?"

John has already started picking his way back uphill, weaving around massive trees and wicked-looking devils claw. "It's hard to say," he finally answers, glancing back over his shoulder to make sure everyone is following. "Tulock pointed out a bare spot almost half-way up the mountain. It's the steepest part, so there aren't nearly as many trees. I figure that if we can reach that before dark, we're making decent time. It shouldn't be that – hey!" he interrupts himself, suddenly stopping.

Sam's head snaps up, assuming their mysterious watcher has returned. But it's obvious that whatever John is now pointing at is a *good* thing. A wide smile lights up his features as he looks back down the hill at them.

"A trail!" he declares, waving his walking stick towards it. "Come on!"

Sam rushes to keep up as everyone gets caught up in the excitement. Rocky begins to bark playfully, tugging at the leash when Sam once again lags behind. Her toes hurt from where they hit the rocks, and her muscles still ache from the deep cold of the water. She has no idea how Ally is doing so well. *Maybe the hit to my head did more than I realized,* she muses. She's looking forward to when they can finally stop for the day.

The five friends gather together to examine the clear remains of what once used to be a rocky pathway. Most of the rocks are either displaced, or reclaimed by the forest. Just enough remain as proof of human construction.

"How do you think this got here?" Hunter asks, rubbing the back of his neck.

"It looks old," Ally adds.

"Ben Shadow."

Everyone looks at Sam in surprise.

"Well, who else would have done it?" Stepping up to the pathway, Sam bends over and picks up one of the stones. "Tulock said that Ben lived on this side of the mountain for years. Wouldn't it make sense that he might make some trails?"

"And a cabin," John adds. "There's supposed to be one around here somewhere. Maybe this leads to it."

"Oh! That would be great," Ally says happily. "I would rather sleep in a cabin, than under the tarp we have!"

"I'll bet it's collapsed by now," Hunter counters. "It's been like, what, over fifty years?"

"Either way," John says while stepping onto the trail. "This means we have a pretty clear path now. It's obviously going up, so we'll follow it for as long as we can. Who knows? Maybe it'll take us all the way to the top!"

Happy to have the way marked out and nearly cleared for them, the group's sprits rise. It feels like the first positive thing that's happened since the plane crash. Cassy even leads them in a couple of camping songs, and Sam is hopeful it will help keep bears or any other animals from getting too close.

After another hour, Sam's legs feel like rubber and her stomach is grumbling. It's getting close to dinnertime, and that means they need to stop soon to make camp before dark. She's about to voice her thoughts when she looks up just in time to avoid walking into Ally. Everyone has stopped and she peeks around her friend to see what's up.

Ahead of them, the woods disappear to reveal a wide strip of treeless terrain, littered with loose rocks and dirt.

"This has to be the spot Tulock showed you," Hunter observes.

Nodding, John doesn't look happy. "It's steeper than I thought it would be." Stepping out onto the old landslide, he looks both above and below them. "This is probably as good a place as any to cross it. But I want to use the two ropes we have to tie off with each other. These rocks have been here a long time, but they're still loose."

They all agree, and within minutes, they're divided into two groups. Hunter, Cassy, and Ally go first, slowly picking their way through the rocks. When they reach the other side without any problems, Sam removes Rocky's leash and has Hunter call him over. The dog is much more agile than they could ever be, and he navigates the obstacle course with ease.

With the shorter rope tied around their waists, John and Sam step out into the open. Sam turns her face up towards the rapidly setting sun, happy to be warmed by it. Looking back to study the slide, she estimates it to be around a hundred feet wide. Larger boulders edge the sides, with the middle holding what appear to be the smallest, most unstable rocks.

They scramble over and around the bigger rocks, and then carefully pick their way through the center, using walking sticks to counter their balance. Sam's left foot slips and she gasps before successfully catching herself. John stops to look back at her and she laughs lightly, brushing off her hands. "I'm fine," she mumbles before he can ask.

Repositioning her stick, Sam becomes aware of an odd sound and pauses to look around. It's like the scurrying of hundreds of mice, and as the sound grows, she notices a stream of dirt and pebbles flowing past her feet.

"Slide!" John shouts.

Panic-stricken, Sam looks up, unsure of which way to go. A cloud of dust is billowing towards them and before she has a chance to react, John wraps her up in a bear hug and throws them both to the ground!

12

SECOND THOUGHTS

"John!" Ally's screams pierce the sudden stillness that follows the roar of the rockslide. "Sam!"

"We're okay!" John calls out from behind a boulder after a horrific moment of silence.

Sam blinks rapidly to clear her eyes of the tears that sting them, as a fierce pain radiates from her right forearm. John's arms loosen around her and then he pushes her back so he can study her face.

"Did any of those rocks hit you, Sam?" he asks quietly. His face is covered in a mask of dirt, his white teeth, and blue eyes standing out amongst the grime.

Sam takes stock, wiggling her fingers and

toes. While her arm hurts, she doesn't think anything is broken. "I'm fine," she replies, and then bursts out laughing. John gives her a quizzical look, making her laugh even harder. "I'm sorry," she gasps, trying to control her irrational reaction. "But you look like a clown, and I laugh when I'm scared."

Pausing, John draws a line with his finger through the mud her tears created on her own face. "Yeah, well, I guess we both look pretty silly *and* scared!" Struggling to his feet, he reaches down to pull Sam up and then they both face their friends who are eagerly watching from nearly thirty feet away.

Sam can see now that John pulled them behind a large rock that protected them from the small slide. She expected to see half the mountain around them, but it's a surprisingly insignificant amount of debris for all the noise it made. However, it would only take one decent sized rock to cause a lot damage. Rubbing gingerly at her arm, Sam shivers slightly. If anything were to happen to them, there's no one out here to call for help.

After taking a couple of slow breaths to calm

their racing hearts, John and Sam carefully make their way across the rest of the expanse. They're greeted by a large group hug that lasts several minutes.

"I want to go home," Cassy moans when they break apart.

Sam looks closely at her friend. The normally confident teen is pale and obviously shaken. She's holding tightly to Ally's hand. Sam has a sudden, almost painful pang of homesickness and has to fight back her own tears. She desperately wants to be safe at home with her parents, but they can't give in to those raw emotions. Not now.

"I know that's not possible," Cassy hastily adds. Placing both hands over her face for a moment she then wipes forcefully at her cheeks to dry them. "But can't we go back to Kerry and Tulock? At least we know we'll be safe there."

"She has a good point," Ally agrees. "This is just too dangerous."

John and Hunter exchange a stoic look. "Look, you guys," John finally says as he removes his backpack. Opening up the top, he digs around in it while continuing to talk. "Going back now means walking back across that rockslide and getting back in the river. We already *know* how risky that is. It's probably safer the rest of the way to the top."

"I can't stop thinking of how we left them alone," Cassy counters. "We should have stayed. What if something happens to Kerry or Riley? What if we don't make it to the top and get lost, or -- "

"Cassy!" Hunter shouts, interrupting her. "We didn't really have a choice. Tulock knew that. That's why he told us *all* to go!"

Cassy blinks, looking in surprise at Hunter and then John. "What do you mean?"

"He means that our best chance of rescue is getting to the top of this mountain," John explains. "I don't mean the *quickest* rescue," John adds when Cassy tries to say something. "I mean being rescued, period. There's no guarantee that the search party is going to find the wreckage. It's tucked down in between two mountain ranges, more than fifty miles north of where it's supposed to be. From the air, there's likely nothing visible, and even if they were to get a signal fire lit, depending on weather and wind, that might not be seen, either."

"*We're* their best chance," Sam tells Cassy. "We can't go back now."

"But you three can stay here," John suggests. Pulling the first aid kit out of his bag John motions for Sam to give him her arm. There's a large welt on the top of her right forearm, and a deep bruise is already starting to develop in the middle of it.

"Can you move your fingers?" he asks.

Nodding, Sam demonstrates her ability, but it's painful. Flexing her hand at the wrist has the same result. "What do you mean, we can stay here?" she asks, more concerned about being left behind, than she is about her arm.

"Cassy is right. This *is* dangerous, but there's no way around it," John explains. "We *have* to keep going to get help, but that doesn't mean all of us have to. We can set up a camp here for the three of you, and Hunter and I will keep going and light the signal fires. This slide would be an easy landmark to find you by."

Sam pulls her arm away from John, who's attempting to put an ace wrap on it. "No!" she exclaims. "We have to stay together!" Looking at Ally with desperation and Cassy, she steps towards them. "We're family, you guys. We can't split up!"

Rocky noses his way in between them, concerned by the tone of Sam's voice. Whimpering, he nudges at her hand. Kneeling down, she wraps her arms around him. Pulling at Cassy, Ally drags the other girl down with her so that all three friends are gathered around the poodle.

"We can do this," Ally urges, looking at first Sam and then Cassy. "If there's one thing Sam has taught me Cass, is that we're stronger than we think we are. We're also stronger when we're together and I don't think it would be smart to split up."

"We'll help you," Sam adds. "You're like our sister now, Cassy. We'd never let anything happen to you!"

Wiping at her nose, Cassy nods silently. Taking a few tentative steps towards the trees, she straightens her shoulders. "We should probably keep following this trail then, right?" she asks, pointing into the woods.

Stepping up next to her, Hunter slaps her loudly on the back. "Good job!" he exclaims happily. "You found it!" Starting up again some twenty feet away is the same, old rocky pathway.

Squinting up at the last remnants of the sun as it slides down behind Shadow Mountain, John swings his pack onto his back. Stepping over to Sam, he finishes wrapping her arm. "You good to go?"

"Yeah," she answers, relieved. "I think I hit it when we fell down. Probably just a bruise."

"So we all go," John decides. When no one objects, he picks up his walking stick and leads the way onto the trail. "Let's follow the path for just a little ways," he suggests. "Maybe we can find a relatively level area to make camp."

Hunter takes up the rear without being asked, much to Sam's relief. Unable to grip her walking stick with her right hand, she's forced to hold both it and Rocky's leash with her left. Without the bear can spray out, she's nervous to be the guard. Hopefully, her arm will be better by tomorrow.

The terrain continues to change the higher they go, and Sam is reminded more and more of the mountains in eastern Washington. A bed of pine needles replaces the moss, the wet damp earthy smell by warming cedar. The ferns aren't as numerous and giant mushrooms don't cling to the fallen trees.

"It's pretty flat over here," Ally points out, pausing next to a huge hemlock.

"I think you'd rather stay up here, instead," John calls back with an edge of excitement in his voice.

Sam scrambles up a steep incline and around an old growth cedar to find John standing in front of an old, weathered lob cabin.

13

SHELTERED

Contrary to Hunter's speculation, the cabin is mostly intact. Unfortunately, the rock fireplace has crumbled, so they're unable to light a fire inside to keep warm. Instead, they make use of the clear area outside and quickly have a large bonfire burning.

Tossing another branch onto the crackling pile, Sam holds her right hand protectively to her chest. She'd forgotten that it was hurt and tried to pick up the kindling with it. She won't make *that* mistake again.

Glancing behind her at the small house, Sam's torn between the comforting warmth of the fire, and her desire to explore it. While John guessed that it's around six, and they should have more than an hour of daylight left, they're already shrouded in darkness. Shadow Mountain stands between them and the setting sun. As soon as it disappeared behind the peak, the temperature began to drop.

"We can boil the water I collected from the river this morning," John states, pulling several plastic bottles of water from his pack. "But if we don't come across any streams tomorrow, we'll need to make this last. How much do you all have left?"

A minute later, there's a collection of empty and half-empty containers on the ground. They add their food to it, then sit back and take stock. There's enough water for two days and food for four, if they carefully ration it out.

"That's the last granola bar you get tonight," John orders while pointing to Hunter. "Didn't you just eat one before we got here? And a peperoni stick?"

"I'm hungry," Hunter answers bluntly. "And there's a whole other box of protein bars," he adds when he sees the scowl cross John's face.

"We're *all* hungry," John replies. Grabbing the mentioned protein bars, he passes them out to the rest of the group. "But there's no guarantee we'll be seen by a plane in another day or two, so we have to be smart about it."

"Maybe there's something in the cabin," Ally suggests.

"You mean a fifty-year-old can of beans?" Hunter retorts. "Sorry," he adds sheepishly, when Ally's eyes widen. "I get mean when I'm hungry."

"You're always mean," Sam mumbles.

"It's okay," Ally sighs. Waving her protein bar towards Hunter, she then takes a bite. "Apology accepted. You're right, anyways," she agrees. "Of course anything left in the cabin by Ben Shadow won't be any good. I guess I was just thinking that some other travelers could have found it throughout the years and maybe stayed there."

"Good idea, sis," John says. "Let's finish boiling the water and re-packing the food and then search it. "Sam," he continues, holding out a hand. "Can you give me your pack? I want to put all the food in it so we can tie it up in a tree. And make sure you don't have anything in your pockets," he adds while staring at Hunter. "Not unless you want a bear waking you up tonight!"

Pulling another granola bar from his back

pocket, Hunter tosses it to John. "It was for my breakfast!"

Laughing at his friend, John then holds out his other hand to Cassy. Looking rather guilty, she takes a peperoni stick from her sweatshirt. Hesitating, she adds a package of trail mix from her jeans before giving them both to John.

"Trail mix?" Hunter says with approval. "You've been holding out on me!"

With the mood notably lightened, Sam helps to re-organize the bags and then supervises as John and Hunter make several attempts at tossing a rope up and over a large branch in a nearby tree. On the fourth toss, it finally lands right and the backpack is soon hoisted up fifteen feet off the ground.

"So, how does putting food in a tree keep bears away?" Cassy asks, standing at the edge of the light emitted from the fire.

"The point isn't to keep them away," John explains. Wiping his hands on his jeans, he tugs on the rope one more time to test it. "The bear's gonna smell it no matter what. The goal is to have it downwind and far enough away so they aren't drawn into the camp. Second, is to have it positioned in the tree so that while they can smell it, they can't get to it."

"Are you sure it's far enough from the cabin?" Ally questions while looking nervously around at the rapidly darkening woods.

Shrugging, John walks back to the fire, followed closely by Hunter and Sam. "Should be. It's getting too dark to go looking for another ideal tree. We'll be fine, Ally," he adds when he sees his sister's worried expression. "Come on, let's go look in the cabin."

Happy to get inside a solid structure with a door, Ally leads the way. It's dark enough to need their flashlights, and several click on at about the same time. The first cursory glance inside when they got there revealed the partially collapsed fireplace and sparse furnishings. Now, they play their lights over the random surfaces, exposing mostly dirt and cobwebs.

"Hey, there's a lantern!" Hunter exclaims. "Do you think the oil in it is still good?"

"Only one way to find out." John steps up next to Hunter at the center pole and pulls out his lighter. The old-fashioned metal and glass lantern is hanging from a nail so that it's positioned in the middle of the cabin. After tugging at the nail to make sure it's secure, John holds the flame to its base. At first, it appears that the wick will simply burn up, but then, with a small flash of ignition, a welcoming light fills the small space.

Surprised at how *normal* the cabin and light make her feel, Sam lets out a breath before sitting down on the nearest ledge. She's suddenly overcome by exhaustion, the events from the day threatening to overwhelm her.

"I don't know how long this oil will last," John is saying, "but we should turn it off before going to sleep, anyways."

The setting revealed by the lantern is like something out of an old western movie. The floor is made of rough-hewn wood, and while a bit uneven, is surprisingly solid. The fireplace was the only source of heat and also likely used for a cooking surface, because there isn't anything else that resembles a kitchen. The only other structures are a small, handmade table with two chairs, and the sleeping platform that Sam sits on.

Sam looks down at the raised platform that's as large as a twin-sized bed. There was likely never a mattress on it and the mice-eaten remnants of a blanket are scattered around. The whole cabin can't be any larger than fifteen by fifteen feet, and Sam wonders what sort of a life Ben Shadow was living in it, alone out here for two whole years.

"No food," Hunter says sadly. He's on his knees, going through two wooden crates pushed up against the wall opposite the fireplace. They appear to be the only form of storage in the cabin. "Just some old rusty tools and what's left of some cardboard boxes. Probably *used* to have food or something useful in them."

"Sixty years is a long time," John says solemnly. "I'm sure that this cabin has been used a few times since Ben disappeared. Anything worthwhile is probably long gone."

Not wanting to leave all the snooping to her brother, Sam forces herself off the 'bed' and squats down next to him. Flashing her light over the items in the crates, she quickly determines that he wasn't exaggerating. A rusted hammer, what looks like a rock pick, and a few other tools take up on of the boxes. The other one is more interesting. Under the broken-down cardboard and chewed up remains is a spiral bound notebook. Feeling a small surge of excitement, Sam pulls it out. A sharpened pencil is jammed in the spine and she slides it through the rings before opening the stiffened pages. Disappointment immediately washes out her enthusiasm. The first two pages had something written on them, but time has erased it to the point of being unreadable. Flipping past them, Sam confirms that the rest of the notepad is blank.

"I think the three of us girls can all fit on here," Ally is saying.

Sam looks up at her friend sleepily to find both her and Cassy huddled on the platform. Nodding in agreement, she stands slowly and then stretches the cramps out of her legs.

"I'll get your stuff," John offers. A few minutes later, he tosses their sleeping bags in at them. "I think Hunter and I will just sleep out here by the fire. It'll be warmer, and we can keep it going to help make sure we don't get any unwanted visitors tonight!"

Too tired to offer any sort of argument, the three girls spread their bags out after sweeping the remains of the blanket off. They barely fit, but manage to make it work.

Normally chatty, Cassy is already asleep by the time Sam turns to tell her goodnight.

Ally is crammed in between them, and she smiles weakly at Sam. "Cassy's phone died."

Before setting out that morning, they'd gone over a plan with Tulock. They all sent the same text message to their parents, with a brief description of what happened and their last known coordinates. Although it's hopeless to even try, not doing it would still be stupid. Since Cassy has a different provider than the rest of them, as well as the most battery left, it was decided that she would leave her phone on first. If they pass through an area with cell service, the text will automatically send. Each of them has been turning their own phones on once an hour, just in case.

"So you're keeping yours on now, right?" Sam confirms.

Nodding, Ally sniffs and then wipes at her nose. "But mine will be dead by the morning." A heavy silence draws out between the two best friends, as they look at each other in the soft glow of the light. "Oh!" Ally gasps. "We forgot to turn the lantern off," she whispers.

Moaning at having to stand up again, Sam knows that she has to do it. Rolling off the edge, she staggers over to the pole. Squinting at the base of the lamp, she frowns. *How in the world do I turn this thing off?* Laughing at herself, she leans in closer. All the lanterns she's ever used have had an on/off switch. Instinct tells her that since there is only one lever on the device that she probably just needs to turn it.

Reaching out for it, she pauses. Just below her hand, on the wooden pole, is what looks like a carving. Leaning in even closer, she can tell that it's a circle with a jumble of lines running through the middle of it, and patterns around the outer ring.

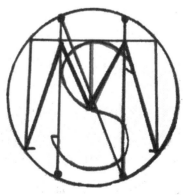

Intrigued, Sam turns to collect the old notepad and pencil from next to her sleeping bag and discovers that Ally is now also fast asleep. Grinning, she goes back to the carving and begins to draw.

14

LEGENDARY ENCOUNTER

The morning comes fast, and Sam wakes up cold.

Wiping at her gummy eyes, she peers at the only window in the cabin and notes the weak, filtered sunlight making its way in. *It must be barely after sunrise*, she guesses.

Her right forearm is now a source of a constant, deep ache. Trying to flex her fingers, Sam's awarded with a sharper pain. She'll need to get some more Ibuprofen. Other than that, she feels surprisingly good. Her head is clearer than the day before, and in spite of the tumble down the river, the strength has returned to her arms and legs.

Trying to snuggle down further in the sleeping bag, Sam can't continue to ignore the pressure in her bladder. Sighing, she's resigned to the fact that she won't be able to fall back asleep. Maybe if she was warm, but her feet are the only part of her body even close to being comfortable, and that's because Rocky is spread out on top of them.

Taking a deep breath as if she's plunging into frigid water, Sam wiggles out of the bed, careful not to wake Ally or Cassy, and then rushes to slip her feet into her nearby shoes. Instantly shivering, she snatches up Rocky's leash and calls quietly to him to follow her outside. After giving her a look that can only be described as disapproving, he leaps to the floor and plods after her.

Happy to find the fire burning high, Sam slips past her snoring brother and sits down next to John. Surprised to find him awake, she looks at him questionably. "Did you sleep at all?"

"On and off," he whispers. "I got a few hours of solid sleep at some point. Thought I heard something earlier, though, so I've been keeping the fire going strong since then. What are *you* doing up so early?"

Reminded of why she came out in the first place, Sam begins fidgeting. Her hands and face are finally warm, and the sun is quickly filling in the open spaces around them. Standing, she hops back and forth on her feet. "I need to find a tree," she explains. "Fast."

Laughing at first, John grows serious when she starts to walk away. "Hey! You shouldn't go alone."

"I'm *not* alone!" Sam replies, holding Rocky's leash up with her left hand. "He'll watch out for me, and I won't go far." Afraid to wait for an answer, Sam spins back around and darts away, the urgency of her condition increasing.

After going twenty feet and around a couple of trees, Sam trips over a rock and nearly falls down. Chastising herself, she takes a moment to look around and discovers the rock is part of another trail! Curiousness momentarily outweighs her distress, and she starts to follow it. It's definitely *not* the same trail that led them to the cabin. It's made differently. Narrower, with the rocks actually arranged in a type of pattern.

After a few minutes, Sam realizes that she's

much further from the cabin than she meant to go. Hesitating, she decides to find a tree first, and then go back and tell John about the trial. It doesn't seem to be going uphill. Stepping into a sudden clearing, Sam studies the round area of low grasses, surrounded by younger cedar trees. It doesn't seem … natural. Shrugging, she walks across it to the nearest tree but then pauses. *The trail is gone,* she thinks, staring at the round patch of ground. The trail obviously was leading to this space for some reason, although she can't imagine why.

"We can figure this out later," Sam mutters under her breath, while dancing a little jig around her chosen tree.

After a few minutes, she's back in the clearing much more relaxed, but also cold. The sun hasn't had a chance yet to warm the chilly air and her breath forms small clouds as she stands with her hands on her hips. "What was Ben Shadow up to out here, Rocky?" she says out loud. The poodle looks up at her and tilts his head. Laughing, Sam reaches out to pet him. "Yeah, I don't know, either. Let's go back and get warm first, then we can show John."

But before Sam can pull her hand back, Rocky shocks her by suddenly baring his teeth and lunging away from her! Stunned, Sam watches as her dog plows through the grass, hackles high, a fierce growl growing in his throat. The leash goes taught just before he reaches the trees.

"Rocky!" Struggling to hold on with her left hand, Sam screams his name and tries to pull him back the opposite direction, towards the trail.

Confused by the unexpected noise and behavior, it takes a moment for Sam to realize that the trees in front of Rocky don't look right. They're moving. Shifting. Coming alive right before her eyes. No! It's not the *trees* that are moving, but something *in* the trees.

A blood-curdling scream builds from deep within Sam but then dies before she can release it as all the air is sucked from her lungs. It's replaced with a cold terror like she's never experienced before. A paralyzing fear that robs her of the ability to move.

Rising up nearly eight feet to tower over her is the largest creature she has ever seen. A giant Kodiak bear, weighing over a thousand pounds.

He paws at the air with claws nearly five inches long. His dark lips quiver and spittle flies towards Sam as he bellows a roar that envelopes her and bounces off the surrounding trees and mountains.

A challenge. One that she will surely loose, and all Sam can think about is her mom. She'll never see her mom again. "Mommy!" she gasps, eyes wide with a feral fear and the knowledge that there is no escape.

The thought compels Sam to move.

Stumbling backwards, she continues to hold Rocky's leash and move clumsily towards the far side of the clearing. Desperate to remember what Tulock told them to do when encountering a bear, her mind is blank, stuck in the fight or flight mode and unable to process complex thoughts. Her vision is narrowed, her breaths coming in quick, ragged gasps in an attempt to keep up with her racing heart.

Taquka-aq paws again towards Rocky, hesitant, apparently confused by the barking. It gives Sam a moment to gather herself, and she freezes, finally remembering that running from the Kodiak is the worst thing to do. She can't outrun him. Taking a deep breath to further clear her head, she feels a burst of hope when her hand goes unconsciously to the bear spray still attached to her jeans.

But she can't get it unhooked.

Whimpering, Sam wills her right hand to work, but her fingers fail to grip the clasp tight enough. Pulling at it with her left hand, while still holding the leash, she fumbles with it. Looking down, distracted, she trips over a log and goes down hard.

Encouraged by her movement the Kodiak falls forward onto all fours and starts to swing its head back forth, grunting, while taking a step towards her.

From her view on the ground, all Sam can see beyond the cinnamon colored head of her beloved dog, is a massive wall of brown fur and bared teeth. Still trying to work the safety cap of the bear spray left-handed, she loses control. A scream that feels as if it's coming from someone else fills the space around her until it's all that she can hear.

15

PECULIAR RESCUE

Silence.

In the abrupt absence of Sam's desperate shrieking, time stands still. Rocky stops barking, left trembling in the shadow of the enormous bear. The Kodiak pauses in his advancement, nostrils flaring as he attempts to smell his prey and determine where to strike first.

Sam knows instinctively that she has moments to live, the realization forcing her into silence and her mind exploding with clarity. A part of her balks at the cliché of it all as brief flashes of snapshots from her past play through her mind. But at the same time, she's is still working the cap off the bottle in her hand.

Then, several things happen at once.

Sam's hand comes up, ready to depress the button in a last frantic attempt at warding off the attack. But beyond the bear, another form emerges from the trees, equal in size and shape. A second, deeper bellow explodes through the clearing, challenging the first bear and causing it to spin around towards it in confusion.

As this is happening, something grabs at the hood of Sam's sweatshirt, launching her off the ground and propelling her backwards through the air. Flailing her arms in a weak attempt to steady herself, she comes down hard on her bottom. As she's dragged onto the rocky path, relief washes over Sam when she sees the Kodiak lumbering away towards the second bear. The opponent is some thirty feet away and standing upright, clawing savagely at a tree trunk.

"Are you hurt, Sam?"

A gruff voice murmurs near Sam's ear and she realizes that a *person* has ahold of her and is attempting to pull her to safety. Rocky is dancing around them, and it dawns on her that he isn't barking at whoever it is. Feeling like she's underwater, Sam looks up at her rescuer and isn't surprised to discover it's John.

"Sam!" he repeats more urgently. "Are you hurt?"

Finally stopping, John lets go of her and steps forward so that he's standing over Sam, staring down into her pale face. "Please answer me," he pleads while looking for any obvious signs of injury. "Did it bite you? Claw you? Sam!"

Shaking her head, Sam tries to clear her thoughts, which are all muddy again. *Why is it so hard to think?* She puzzles, frowning. Looking back at John, she's jolted by the fear she sees. "I'm okay," she manages to whisper. "I'm okay. I'm okay. I'm okay." Breaking down in sobs as she continues to repeat her declaration, she allows John to help her to her feet.

"We have to get out of here," he urges, unsure how to handle her emotional breakdown.

"Sam! John!" Hunter appears on the trail, running recklessly. "What was that *sound*? It woke me up! Was it a bear? I thought I heard screaming, too!"

"Go back!" John orders, already guiding Sam by the shoulders in that direction. "We've got to go back, now!"

Each boy taking an arm, they nearly carry

Sam towards the cabin as fast as they can go. A short distance from the fire, they run into Ally and Cassy, who were also woken by Sam's screams.

A hand flying to her mouth, Ally jumps back out of the boy's way. Grabbing at Cassy, she holds on to her arm with a vise-like grip. "What happened to her?" she demands. When no one answers, she moves to hover over Sam, who now slumps down in front of the fire, furtively looking back towards the trail. "John!" Ally yells at her brother, alarmed by Sam's behavior. "Talk to me!"

"I think she's in shock," he replies curtly. "Go get a sleeping bag," he orders, pointing at the cabin. "And Hunter," he adds, tossing his can of bear spray at him. "Stay over there by the trail and let us know if you hear *anything* moving this way."

Unusually quiet, Hunter catches the can and moves back swiftly to the head of the trail. Whistling at Rocky, he calls the dog over and picks up the leash he's trailing behind him. Once in position to stand guard, he crosses his arms and stares back at his sister, his brows drawn together in a heavy scowl.

"It *was* a bear!" Cassy gulps. "Oh, Sam!" Sitting down next to her friend, she wraps an arm around her shoulder. Looking back up at John for answers, Cassy is further troubled by his demeanor. Normally confident, he's noticeably nervous and jumpy.

"There were two bears," he explains to the group when Ally reappears with a sleeping bag. Helping her drape it around Sam, he then steps back and crosses his arms over his chest. "I was already halfway down the trail when I heard you scream, Sam. When you stopped -- "

"I was too scared to scream anymore," she explains, trying to laugh it off and failing miserably. Instead of a chuckle, a mix between a sob and moan escapes. When she tries to stop the sound, it only gets worse, until she's openly crying. Embarrassed, Sam buries her face in Cassy's shoulder. Ally sits on her other side and they all huddle together.

When her tears finally dry up, Sam feels much better, but incredibly tired. Her shivering stopped and her stomach has settled down. She seriously thought she would throw up there for a while. The whole encounter is already taking on a sort of nightmare effect ... like it didn't really happen. "I just had to go to the bathroom." Sitting up straight, she looks around at her friends and brother. "Good thing I found the tree before the bear found me, or else I'd have to change my pants."

There's a moment of heavy silence before Cassy disrupts it with a loud snort. The tension broken, they all start laughing, thankful for the release.

"You should go lay down," Ally suggests, when she sees Sam yawing for the third time.

"In a nice, solid cabin with a door to keep bears out," Cassy adds.

Surprising everyone, Sam agrees. "I *did* wake up early," She states. Standing slowly and holding the sleeping bag around her awkwardly with one hand, she shuffles towards the cabin. "Just for a little while."

***

Two hours later, Sam stumbles back out of the cabin. Looking sheepishly at her friends gathered around the now-smoldering fire, she accepts a bottle of water before sitting next to Ally.

"Sorry, guys. I didn't mean to sleep that long!"

"It's the best thing you could have done, after what happened," John says. "How are you feeling?"

Shrugging, Sam takes a long drink. "I'm really okay. But I might have nightmares for a while! I'm sorry to make us get such a late start."

"It's barely eight," Hunter tells her. "We should be able to reach the top before dark without any trouble. We ended up making really good time yesterday. But -- "

"What?" Sam asks, when Hunter pauses and looks at John.

"The direction we need to go is where those bears were," John explains pointing towards the trail. "But I don't think we need to worry about them," he adds in a rush. "Last I saw, that second bear was chasing the first one in the opposite direction, and Hunter and I just went back to the clearing a few minutes ago and there's no sign of them."

Doing her best to hide her fear, Sam nods slowly. "The path ends in that circle of grass, and I didn't see it start up again anywhere. Do you think Ben created it? What would be the point?"

"Who knows," Cassy replies. "He was basically a hermit up here. Maybe he cleared out a spot to sunbathe."

Laughing, Ally stands up and starts kicking dirt on the remains of the fire. "Or maybe for star gazing? Or he could have even had a garden there at some point, and it's just long overgrown."

"I'll bet you're right!" Sam agrees. "That makes the most sense." Joining Ally in snuffing out the fire completely, she grabs a stick to stir at the remaining coals.

Once all signs of it are gone, they all busy themselves with getting their packs organized, including Sam's, which they already retrieved in order to eat something for breakfast.

Sam's thankful when John swaps out all of the food from her backpack for other items. She really doesn't want to have the bear bait strapped to her! Turning to look one last time at the cabin, Sam wonders if they'll ever see it again. Probably not, unless the signal fires don't work and they aren't rescued. Then they might end up having to come back. Shaking her head at the thought, she falls in behind Ally, with Hunter behind her.

It takes less than ten minutes to reach the opening and they make sure to talk loudly and bang their walking sticks. Thankfully, the space is empty of bears.

"We need to go that way." John is standing with his compass out, pointing in the general direction where the second bear had been. "Due west. Hopefully we'll soon be high enough that it'll open up more and we can actually *see* the summit."

Everyone follows John without comment. The trees thicken around them again, and they continue to hit at them with their walking sticks to help ward off any bears.

As Sam passes the tree that the Kodiak was scratching at, she pauses to run her fingers along the deep grooves left in the bark. She has to reach over her head and is amazed at how powerful the animal had to be to leave so much damage behind on the large cedar. Shuddering, she steps back and happens to see something else in the bark at eye-level. Curious, she leans in. Eyes widening, she quickly starts removing her backpack.

"What are you doing?" Ally asks, concerned by Sam's odd behavior. Maybe she really isn't okay after all.

Pulling the old notebook out that she found in the Cabin, Sam flips it open to the drawing she made of the carving on the post. Holding it next to the mark on the tree, she smiles widely at Ally. "It's the same!" she exclaims.

Confused, Ally looks back-and-forth between the two symbols. "I don't understand."

"This *same* carving was on the post in the cabin!" Sam explains, realizing that Ally probably didn't notice it. "Ben Shadow put this here, and I'll bet he did it for a reason!"

16

BREADCRUMBS

"What are you looking at?" Hunter stops next to the two girls and puts his hands on his hips. "It's called a tree. With scratch marks on it."

Sam rolls her eyes at her brother. "There was a carving on the post back in the cabin."

"Yeah, so what? I saw it. Didn't really make any sense."

"Look!" Sam demands, holding the notebook back up again.

"Uh-huh. So Ben Shadow liked to whittle. Can we go now? I don't want to stick around here any longer than we have to." Hunter looks back over his shoulder while he's talking.

"They're not quite the same," Ally observes,

ignoring Hunter.

"Hmmm … " Sam turns her drawing until the symbols all line up. "You're right. The one on the tree is rotated. There are marks under it, too."

X V I I

"Those are called roman numerals, brainiac." In spite of Hunter's complaining, he steps back up to the tree to have a closer look. "The X, V, and two II's mean twenty seven."

"Twenty seven what?" John asks as he and Cassy join them.

"We don't know," Ally answers. "Sam found this carving here on the tree, and I guess the same one – well, *almost* same one was also in the cabin. She think's Ben Shadow put it here."

"It looks like a W," Cassy points out.

Sam tilts her head to the side, studying the lines within the circle on the bark. Letting out a small cry, she steps back and holds the notebook out. "Cassy! You're right. That *is* a W. Look!" Rotating the page with the drawing first to the left and then slightly to the right, she waits for the others to catch on.

"It's directions." John is the first to speak. "Like a compass. Great find, Sam!"

"Wait." Hunter puts his hands up. "I see it now. W, S, E, N. You think those stand for west, south, east, and north?"

"Oh! I get it!" Ally runs her finger along the outline of the W, the letter currently upright in the circle on the tree. So this is like a marker? Then what about the numbers under it?"

"Paces." John is already putting his back up against the opposite side of the tree, and then begins to walk away in a straight line, counting under his breath.

"Oh, my gosh," Hunter mumbles. "Does no one else care that we're still standing in like, giant killer bear territory? How do you even know that's what it's for?"

"We'll find out soon enough!" Sam calls out as she grabs Ally and they chase after John.

Hanging his head, Hunter allows Cassy to push him in the same direction. It doesn't take long to go the twenty-seven paces and they catch up with the other three at the base of a giant Hemlock.

"It's here!" John announces. "The same carving, but this time the S is the one aligned vertically."

"Two-hundred steps. South is to our left?" Cassy holds her hand out while she's speaking; pointing in the general direction the bears went.

Nodding is response; John is already taking off again.

"Hold up!" Hunter calls out. "Aren't we getting off track now?"

"We won't take more than ten minutes or so," John agrees. "If it doesn't turn back west, then we'll stop following it. Sound good?" He includes everyone in the question, and they all agree.

It only takes five minutes before the next mark is located, and it again turns them back west. This time, it's for three hundred paces and they all trudge uphill in silence. When John stops ten minutes later, he stands looking around in confusion.

"I don't see any obvious, large trees," Ally says.

"At least if there isn't anything here we're still going in the right direction," Cassy offers.

Sam goes to the nearest Cedar and walks around its base, Rocky sniffing alongside her. Not finding anything, she climbs over a log and moves onto the next one a few feet ahead of it, with the same result.

Hunter looks up at the sun, nearly directly overhead. "I hate to be negative you guys, but how much time are we going to waste?" Slipping a water bottle out of a side pocket on his pack, he takes a long swallow. Raising it for another drink, he hesitates, noticing that it's half-empty. The day is already much warmer than the previous two, and they're going through the water too fast. "We need to find a stream."

Looking at her brother, Sam sits down on the log. She knows he's right. Thanks to her wandering off this morning and nearly being attacked by the bear, they've already lost a lot of time. Looking down at her feet, she kicks at the bark behind her heels and then freezes. Smiling, she spins around and squats down in front of the fallen spruce. "Found it!" she calls out. "Only thirty paces to the north this time."

John follows the tree to its bared roots and starts off to the north. Hunter is the last to fall in without comment.

Two hours later, the five have hiked in a generally western direction, making steady progress uphill. The markers vary from only a handful of steps to several hundred, with the longer stretches always leading them towards the summit.

Sam makes another mark in her notebook as they set off for a hundred steps west again. She counts the entries as she walks behind Ally. "This is the thirty-fifth one, Ally!"

Ally pauses long enough to come alongside Sam, and hooks a hand through her arm in a familiar gesture. "What do you think it's all for?"

Sam studies her best friend for a moment, considering how they came to be in the middle of the Alaska wilderness, following clues left by a young miner over fifty years ago. Shaking her head, she suppresses the more depressing thoughts of Tulock and whether they'll be able to get help in time. This distraction is good, and even if it doesn't lead to anything, it's still helping to get them to their destination.

"I'm not sure, Ally," she finally says as they stop near where John and Hunter are looking for the next carving. Hunter has finally gotten into the whole thing, once they were able to see the summit and knew they were going the right way. "Based on what Tulock said, the only things that mattered to Ben Shadow was his girlfriend, Auka, and the gold."

"Fifty paces north," Cassy states, coming to stand with Ally and Sam.

"Sam thinks it's going to lead us to the gold," Ally whispers.

As Cassy's eyes widen, Sam purses her lips. "I didn't exactly say that. I just said that's what was important to Ben. What else would he leave a secret trail to?"

"Well, hopefully not his meeting spot with Taquka-aq. Remember, he claimed to speak with the bear in person!"

Sam stares open-mouthed at Cassy as she

races back to walk with Hunter. Risking a glance at Ally, she cringes at her expression. "Cassy's joking!" but in spite of her encouragement, Sam holds a little more tightly to Rocky's leash. She knows now that she can trust her dog's instincts for bears.

The group drops down over a small rise and finds themselves in a shaded gulch; a deep, V-shaped valley formed by erosion into the mountainside. Through its middle, a small stream gurgles. John and Hunter immediately begin filling the empty water bottles.

Walking slowly along the sparse trees hugging the rock-face of the valley, Sam marvels at the distinct difference between the woods above and this small, separate ecosystem. She's so enthralled with the patterns of the exposed rock in contrast to the thick grass covering the floor of the valley, that she nearly misses the next marker. It's larger than the others are, and is carved into the rock itself, instead of a tree.

"Guys! Over here!" Sam is already drawing it into the notebook, along with the instructions of sixty paces west, which takes them across the steam and to the other side.

Taking their shoes off, they wade through the ice-cold but refreshing water, and then gather along the base of the cliff face. Spreading out, they begin searching.

After several minutes, Sam is beginning to think this might be the end of their luck. There doesn't appear to be another carving anywhere. Approaching a grove of stunted trees that are likely much older than they look, she attempts to push her way through the foliage but comes up short.

There's something strange about it. Stepping back, she hesitates and then tugs at a clump of overhanging moss and ferns. They fall away to reveal a rough, but definitely manmade structure.

"A door!" Sam calls out triumphantly. "I've found a door!"

17

HEART OF THE
MOUNTAIN

Sam hesitates at the threshold to Ben Shadow's mine. The memory of the last time she and Ally ventured into one a year ago at Hollow Inn left a lasting impression. A cool breeze escapes from the cavernous darkness, billowing the loose hair that escaped her ponytail about her face. Goosebumps rise on her arms and she's quite certain that they're about to make an important discovery. Clicking on a flashlight she takes from a pocket on the waist strap of her backpack, Sam looks to John questioningly as he steps up next to her.

"Hold up, Sam. We have no idea if this old mine is safe to go in." In spite of his concern,

John takes out his own flashlight and begins examining the entrance.

"It's not really a mine."

They both turn to look at Ally in surprise.

"Well, at least not the kind you're thinking of." Taking Sam's flashlight, Ally moves up closer to the rough rock surface. "Remember what Tulock said about the mining around here? They either pan for it, or do the hard rock mining, where they find a gold vein in a mountain and use a pickaxe to dig it out. To actually build a tunnel like this would take a ton of work with a bunch of people and equipment. There aren't any wooden beams for support, either. I'm sure this is just a cave that Ben Shadow found and then explored, looking for the gold veins that naturally occur."

"Since when did you become an expert?" Hunter asks. Sitting down on a boulder, he removes one of his shoes and begins rubbing his foot.

Blushing, Ally crosses her arms over chest defensively. "After going into that mine at Hollow Inn, I got curious and read up on them. It's pretty basic stuff, Hunter. I'm sure you could even understand it."

Sam turns an approving smile towards Ally. "Nice," she whispers. "She's got to be right," she says to John. "This totally looks like it's just a cave. A *big* cave," she adds, trying to shine her light inside.

"Well, it's definitely less likely to be dangerous if it's a natural cave," John admits. "But I still don't see why we should take the time or risk going inside."

"How can we *not?*" Sam pleads. "Ben Shadow led us here. He wanted it to be found!"

Hunter rolls his eyes and then slips his shoe back on. "Don't be so dramatic, sis. But I'm up for checking it out. We spent half the day following those stupid carvings. Doesn't make much sense to stop now. What if there's gold in there?"

"I don't care what's inside," Cassy states. "It's freaky."

John has taken several steps inside the cave and is silently shining his light around at the walls that extend up well above his head. Seeing something, he goes further into the darkness and then there's a sudden flash of additional light.

"There are lanterns on the wall in here!" he calls back.

Not waiting for a formal declaration to explore, Sam and Ally sprint in after him. About twenty feet in, there is a large nail hammered into the rock face of the cave with a glass lamp hanging off it, similar to the one in the cabin.

"I can just make out another one up there," John says pointing with his flashlight.

Sam looks around at the natural cave in awe. The entrance is more of a cavern. It has to be close to twenty feet high and forty feet wide. The ceiling curves down slowly towards the ground in the back, until it turns into more of tunnel that's roughly eight feet high and five feet wide. This is where the first lantern is situated, and it's clear that this is the way to go.

The three of them stand looking at each other in the dim light. A steady splashing sound from a far corner indicates a water source, but other than that, the cave is eerily quiet.

"Well, what are we waiting for?"

Sam didn't hear Hunter walking up behind her and she jumps several inches at the sound of his voice. She joins the others in laughing at herself, and it breaks the slow tension that was building.

"As soon as there aren't any more lanterns, I'm going back." Cassy is clinging tightly to Hunter's arm, looking beyond him down the darkened tunnel with wide eyes.

"We all stick together," John says decisively. Running a hand through his hair, he hesitates for a moment before moving beyond the lamp.

Needing to hold the flashlight, Sam passes Rocky's leash to Ally. The poodle appears relaxed, sniffing eagerly at every rock that they pass. As he nudges at one, she suddenly freezes and gasps. "Snakes! Are there rattlesnakes in Alaska?"

Remembering their close encounter with the rattlesnake, Ally nearly stumbles. Grabbing for her brother, she latches onto John.

Laughing, John tries to remove his sister's vise-like grip. "Don't worry, guys, I distinctly remember reading that the only snake in Alaska is the garter snake. Seriously," he adds, when Ally continues to create grooves in his skin. "It's well-known for it. It's too cold up here year-round for them."

Adequately convinced, Ally moves back to Sam's side and they exchange a knowing grin. They might make a lot of mistakes, but they try to learn from them.

Another source of light comes to life as John finds the next lantern. It reveals more of the same scenery, except that now there are several spots along the wall where someone was obviously digging. While most of the holes are only inches deep, there are a couple that extend several feet.

Sam pauses at one of the bigger spots of excavation and shines her light inside. Nothing sparkles. Pulling her head back out, she wonders how long it would have taken for Ben to create it.

"Can you imagine being alone in here for months, digging all day long?" Ally says softly.

Sam glances at her friend and tries to picture what it must have been like. She can almost hear the pickaxe striking against rock, the sound echoing through the chambers. Goosebumps prickle her arms again, this time tracing a pathway to the nape of her neck. The cave has an odd atmosphere to it, compelling them to speak quietly and tread lightly, almost like they were trespassing in a church.

"I don't like it in here." Cassy has freed herself from Hunter and settles in between Ally and Sam. The three of them loop their arms together and begin to walk three abreast down the tunnel.

"It does have a sort of horror movie kind of feel to it," Ally admits.

"You mean the one where you yell at them to stop, and wonder why in the world they would keep going?" Hunter says playfully as he edges past them to join John.

Sam watches as the two boys are turned into a silhouette by another lamp flaring up. They've come nearly a hundred feet inside the cave, and she's surprised that John hasn't stopped them. Perhaps he also has a sense that they're close to something important.

"It turns to the left here," John calls out. "And it's starting to narrow. We'll need to go back if it doesn't end soon."

No one disagrees and they continue their exploration in silence, except for the occasional whine or playful bark from Rocky.

Sam notices that the floor has begun to tilt

slightly downward. Didn't Tulock say that gold veins often run through the heart of a mountain? The direction of the tunnel is now leading them to the center of Shadow Mountain.

The girls catch up with Hunter and John as they near where the light of the lamp meets the absolute blackness of the cave beyond. Stopping, John begins searching along the walls to see if there is another lantern.

Sam is beginning to think that they're at the end of the quest, when she hears the distinct sound of John's lighter striking. It's followed by the rewarding glow of light pushing back the inky shadows.

But before Sam has a chance to see what it's revealed, John lets out a holler and recoils back into Hunter. Alarmed, she turns to where John is soundlessly pointing.

On the ground is an odd, misshapen pile of dirty furs. Poking out from under it is the unmistakable skeletal remains of a human hand.

They've found Ben Shadow.

18

LAST WISHES

It takes a moment before everyone grasps what they're looking at. As comprehension floods Ally, she lets out a shriek and reels backwards, colliding with Sam and Cassy. The three end up in a heap on the dirt floor, mere feet from the source of their panic.

Now at eye-level with the remains, Cassy also cries out in alarm and scoots backwards in the dirt. Rocky, excited more by the noise than the skeleton, jumps around them and barks eagerly.

"Oh man, that's just wrong," Hunter moans. In spite of his aversion, he leans in closer for a better look. "What's left of the fur coat is all torn up and matted, like with blood or something. Has to be Ben, don't you think?"

John has recovered from his shock and already has his pack off. Nodding in reply, he silently pulls out the first aid kit and rummages around in it until he finds a silver emergency blanket.

"Pretty sure that isn't going to help."

John frowns at Hunter's poor attempt at a joke and respectfully covers the remains with the sheet of cellophane. When Rocky suddenly notices the odd object, he nearly starts digging at it before John can pick him up. Holding the poodle, he looks at the rest of the group with raised eyebrows.

Sam is the first of the girls to recover. Standing slowly, she brushes the dirt from her jeans and edges up next to John and Rocky. Curiosity overcomes her squeamishness and she moves forward to beyond Ben's head. "There's something here!" she exclaims almost immediately. "Some sort of book."

Hunter shines a flashlight at Sam's feet, revealing a large, leather-bound book. Squatting down, Sam warily reaches for it, all too aware of the skeletal hand mere inches from her own. Picking it up, she's surprised by its weight. The leather binding is thick and the paper course. Opening the cover, she immediately sees that it's nothing more than columns of notes, weights, and dollar amounts.

"I'm guessing that Ben kept track of the gold he took into town with this," John suggests, looking over Sam's shoulder.

Pointing at a doubled underscore towards the bottom of the page, Hunter squints to read it. "Huh. Looks like Ben wasn't happy with the results. You think the percentage is like, the purity of the gold or something? I learned that from a TV show," he adds, although no one asked.

"If it is, then it's no wonder he stayed up here and kept looking," Sam observes. Flipping halfway through the book, she stops at the last set of numbers. "1957. Ten ounces, and he only got paid eighty dollars for it. Geeze. That would hardly be enough for food, right?"

"I don't know much about the price of gold, but eight dollars an ounce is like, horrible. Even that long ago. Last year when I looked up, it was over a thousand an ounce," Ally states. She's keeping her distance with Cassy. They're both on their feet, but staying back just inside the reach of the last lantern.

"Wait, there's one more entry here," Sam mutters, noticing a leather tassel marking a page further back. One neat row of numbers is carefully printed across the top, and then a shaky script is scrawled across the rest.

"Six hundred and thirty dollars for eighteen ounces!" Hunter exclaims. "Looks like Ben hit the payload."

"This is a note to Auka," Sam whispers.

"What?" Cassy questions. "What do you mean a note?"

"Ben wrote a message to Auka before he died. He -- " Sam swallows hard. It doesn't feel right to read the obviously private message, so she sums it up. "He apologizes for choosing the mountain over her. But if she can find it in her heart to forgive him, he would forever be at peace. He says something about hoping she used the symbol contained in his last letter to find the cave, and then …. then, it looks like he drew a map!"

John gives Rocky to Hunter and then takes the ledger from Sam, scrutinizing the rugged drawing. Finally nodding, he looks up and points down the tunnel, deeper into Shadow Mountain. "This goes on for quite a ways. According to this, the gold vein he last tested is at the heart of it."

A silence surrounds them as they each consider what it means. After a minute, Sam takes the book back from John and closes it with resolve. "Tulack said his great aunt is still alive. We should take this to Auka so she can decide what to do with it."

"What about Ben?" Hunter asks. "Should we, like, bury him or something?"

"He's been entombed in here for over fifty years already," John replies. "I think we should let him rest, and Auka can decide if she wants to have him buried, *or* if she wants the location of the gold revealed."

Sam looks down at her feet to make sure she avoids stepping on Ben's outstretched hand that didn't quite fit under the blanket and notices something shiny when Hunter's flashlight passes over it. Squatting back down again she sees a silver, oval shape partially covered in the dirt. Digging at it with a finger, Sam uncovers a locket and when she picks it up, the dainty chain attached to it leads back to Ben's fingers. Hesitating, she tugs gently and thankfully, the necklace comes free.

"What'd you find?" Ally has hung back from the rest of the group to wait for Sam and now reluctantly edges closer.

"A locket!" Sam exclaims. "I just have to figure out … ah-ha!" With a barely audible snap, the locket pops open to reveal a small, faded black and white image of a beautiful Inuit woman holding the arm of a tall, skinny white man. "All my love, Auka," Sam reads, squinting to decipher the small letters inscribed opposite the picture.

"Oh!" Ally gasps, holding her hand out to help Sam to her feet. Taking the locket from her friend, she steps closer to the lantern to read it for herself. "What should we do with it?" Twirling the jewelry in her fingers nervously, she looks down at what remains of Ben Shadow and then back to where the rest of the group is fading into the next swath of light thirty feet away.

Scrunching her brows together in thought and pursing her lips, Sam taps at her chin. "What if that's the *only* picture they took together? I think Ben would want her to have it. In fact,"

Sam adds her eyes widening for emphasis as she looks at her best friend, "I'm sure Ben *wanted* us to find him!"

"Well, of course he wanted *someone* to find the mine," Ally agrees. Tilting her head at her friend's odd choice of words, she does her best to reel her imagination in. "I think, that based on what he wrote in the ledger, it's pretty clear he left the symbol as a clue for Auka at some point. She either didn't figure it out, or didn't want to look for this place."

"No," Sam replies while shaking her head emphatically. "I mean that Ben went out of his way to make sure *we* found this place today, so we could bring this all back to Auka and finally put him at rest." When Ally stares at her in disbelief, Sam takes ahold of her arms for emphasis. "Think about it! How likely is it that another bear is going to show up at just the right time and *chase* after another Kodiak! Oh, and that was after he happened to mark the tree with the first clue on it. Remember the legend, Ally!"

"Sam, you don't *really* believe that bear was Ben Shadow!"

"I guess it doesn't matter what I think," Sam

replies, stepping back and holding up the necklace. "But Taquka-aq led us here."

"But it's just a legend," Ally presses.

Sam doesn't respond, reaching out towards the lantern to extinguish the light. But before she can grasp the knob, a cold blast of air billows up from deep inside the mountain, slams into them, and swings the lamp so violently that the oil sloshes over the wick, snuffing it out.

19

SUMMIT

"Still think this is all a coincidence?"

Ally fidgets nervously with the hem of her t-shirt as she follows Sam through the entrance to the cave and back out into the bright daylight. Relieved, she turns to watch Sam secure the door. "I don't know *what* I think, Sam. I'm just glad to be out of there and on our way again."

Tucking the necklace into the front pocket of her jeans, Sam takes Ally's hand and they push their way back through the foliage concealing the cave. Cassy is waiting for them a few feet away near the stream. "It doesn't matter," Sam repeats looking up at the far side of the ravine. John waves at them before he and Hunter start to climb up. "Either way, we should be at the summit before dark and that much closer to being rescued!"

"Hurry up, you guys!" Cassy is waving them over, looking anxiously at the retreating boys. "John wants to go back and get something from the last marked tree, so I told him I'd wait for you. Why'd you take so long? You couldn't pay me to spend one extra second in that place!"

Rocky barks for emphasis, pulling at the leash Cassy is holding. Happy to let go of it, Cassy releases him so he can pounce on Sam. Laughing, Sam kneels down to allow her furry friend to lick her face.

"Sam found a necklace!" Ally explains. "It's a locket with a picture of Auka and Ben."

"Huh," Cassy replies. "Cool, I guess, but still not enough to keep me in there! And I *really* want to catch up with the guys," she adds. "Don't you think this looks like prime bear country?"

Sam suddenly looks at the picturesque setting in a different light. Cassy might be right. The stream running through the middle is deep enough to have fish in it, and it's the first source of water they've seen all day. The sun is high overhead now, warming the forest floor to emit the sweet, natural smells that permeate the woods.

When Sam spots a cluster of raspberry bushes nearby, her stomach clenches. Contrary to the popular belief that bears are meat-eaters, most of their diet is made up of berries. Her encounter from the morning flashes to the front of her mind and sweat instantly springs on her forehead. Her heart skips a beat before doubling its cadence and she fumbles to remove the bear spray from her waist. Rocky, sensing her change in demeanor whines while looking up at her with his intelligent, brown eyes.

"Here." Sam hands the canister to Cassy as she passes by on her way to the stream. "I've already proven that I can't use it."

After quickly removing their shoes, the girls rush across the shallow water. They've barely reached the top of the canyon when first John and then Hunter return. John's holding a palm-sized piece of bark in his hand.

"What's that?" Ally accepts her brother's hand to pull her up over the last rise.

"It's the symbol!" Sam guesses. "The last

one. With that gone, it'll be nearly impossible for anyone to find the cave."

"Anyone except who it was intended for," John adds. Opening the ledger, he carefully places the bark inside and then closes it. "Turn around, Sam."

Sam complies without question and feels the extra weight of the book in more ways than one as John stuffs it into her backpack.

"This is touching and all, but can we *please* find the top of this cursed mountain?" Hunter doesn't wait for an answer and is already walking away. "This way, right?" Pausing, he looks back at John.

Laughing, John takes Hunter by the shoulders and steers him in a different direction. "This way, Christopher Columbus."

The mood is more subdued as they begin their final leg of the journey. Concern for Tulock and worried family occupy their thoughts. The unspoken question of whether or not they've missed the search plane hangs between them.

"I can't believe it's only been three days since the plane crashed," Cassy comments after nearly an hour of silence. "It feels like we've been out here for weeks!"

"What day is it?" Ally asks.

"Monday," John answers without hesitating. "Two nights since we crashed."

Sam reflects once again on how her brush with death was just that morning. It feels far away, and she supposes it's part of a coping mechanism, with brief flashes of terror and dreams sneaking their way out every once in a while. "Do you think Mom is here, Hunter? In Alaska, I mean."

Hunter pauses, but without answering, he shrugs and then pushes on.

Understanding that it's too hard to talk about, Sam lets it go. The only thing they can control is what they're doing right now. Grabbing onto that thought, she pushes her tired legs even harder. They should reach the summit anytime now.

It turns out to be another two hours.

Just when it looks like the sun is going to leave them in the dark before they reach their goal; they break free of the woods and find themselves looking at a broad, grassy knoll. Giant rocks sprout from the top, with narrow pathways running in between them. To either side of them taller peaks tower, still capped with snow. If the sun were higher in the sky, they would be cast in their shadows, giving the mountain its namesake.

"We made it!" Ally grabs Sam and Cally's hands, running with them out into the open.

Throwing his pack thankfully to the ground, Hunter smiles for the first time in hours. "Woo-hoo!" Hollering at the top of his lungs, he slaps John hard on the back. "We did it, man!"

John smiles in response, and then laughs at Rocky as he prances around them all before rolling happily in the grass, probably in something smelly. Although relieved, he is slower to remove his backpack. Studying the clearing, he picks out the best spots to build their fires. It's already quickly approaching twilight, and with a waning moon, their only light tonight will be the stars. "We've got to start collecting firewood. Fast."

Sam detects the urgency in John's voice and understands immediately. They can't find the needed wood in the dark. If the fires aren't built by morning, they could miss a plane, if they haven't already.

Pulling her hand away from Ally, she takes off her own pack. "Come on!" leading the way, she heads for the nearest deadfall.

Within half an hour, night is upon them. They have three decent sized piles of wood, and one smaller one for their campfire.

"We'll need to get more in the morning," John observes. Frowning, he walks between the three unlit bonfires for the third time, making sure the strips of tire are set out near the kindling at the bases. "But this will have to do for now. We'll get our campfire lit and then be sure to keep it going, so we can use it to set fire to the rest at a moment's notice."

Eager for both the warmth and protection of the fire, the five of them huddle around it with their flashlights. When John fails to produce a flame right away, Sam shines her light on him. Her stomach drops at what she reveals. Frantic with worry, John is dumping the contents from his backpack.

"I can't find it," he mutters, rummaging through his things on the ground. "My lighter is gone!"

THE LEGEND OF SHADOW MOUNTAIN

20

SIGNALS

"How could I be so stupid?" Kicking at a bottle of water, John pats down all of his pockets again. "The last time I used it was to light the lamp in the cave. I think I might have dropped it when I saw Ben, and didn't even realize it."

"Where's your flint?" Ally asks quietly of her brother. She's never seen him so distraught.

"I left it with Kerry in case their lighter ran out of fluid. I figured they'd be more likely to need it." Starting to pace, John stops himself and takes a deep breath. "Okay. Panicking isn't going to help. Our only option is to do this the old-fashioned way."

"You mean by rubbing two sticks together?"

Hunter ads his flashlight to Sam's so that John puts a hand up to shield his eyes. "I know you're a boy scout and all, but have you ever actually started a fire that way?"

"Once," John says hesitantly. "It took a lot of prime, dry kindling and about four hours with six of us sweating over it."

"Sounds great," Cassy moans.

"Or, we could just use *my* flint." Sam kneels down next to her bag and digs until she finds her small emergency kit in the bottom. "Yes!" she exclaims when she pulls out the striking stone. "I wasn't positive it was in here. Thank goodness I always keep it in my bag."

Relief flooding his face, John sits down hard on the ground. "Sweet! I really didn't want to test my fire-making skills. You do the honors, Sam."

Sam strikes at the stone while Ally and Cassy blow at the small sparks that fly out onto a mound of dry moss. In less than a minute it's smoking, and they all cheer when it flashes into a bright flame. Feeding first small sticks and then larger ones to the growing fire, Sam then carefully leans more significant branches over the top to create a tepee.

"Perfect!" Nodding in approval, John high-fives Sam. "I couldn't have done it better myself. I'll take the first watch," he adds. "I doubt that anyone will be out searching at night, but you never know. There could be someone flying over that's on their way to Ketchikan. We have to be pretty close to the normal flight path here."

"I'll take the second watch," Hunter offers.

Sam is still blushing from the praise as she spreads her sleeping bag out in between Ally and Cassy. Even with the fire, it's going to be a cold night under the starry sky.

Doubting that she'll be able to fall asleep, Sam pulls the sleeping bag over her head and tries to push any scary thoughts from her mind. It feels like she's starting to be pulled under the dark waters of sub consciousness when her brother's voice roughly pulls her back.

"A plane! Everyone wake up, I hear a plane!"

Jerking awake with a start, Sam bolts upright to discover it's early dawn. Dew has settled on the glen and her sleeping bag is heavy with it. Her eyes sticky with sleep, she searches for her brother, and sees him racing across the clearing with a burning stick in his hand.

"Come on!" Hunter yells urgently to them. "We're going to miss it!"

John is the first on his feet and he snatches another large stick from the nearby campfire. Sam follows suite and is soon staggering behind them, her own burning torch in hand.

In the distance, a low droning sound is building in intensity.

Looking down at her feet, Sam notices that there's a layer of fog. Her head snaps up and she's dismayed to see that it extends into the nearby trees. In her years of camping, she's used to the phenomenon. It can often take hours of sunlight before the dampness from the night is completely chased away. It means they'll have to get the fires built even higher in order to be seen.

"It isn't going to be enough!" John has come to the same conclusion and is frantically blowing on his signal fire, trying to make it burn faster.

"Here!" Ally runs up to Sam with another burning stick. Behind her, Cassy is taking one to John.

The sound of the plane becomes more distinct, driving them all to work desperately. Rocky begins to bark. Sam nearly trips over him as she sprints back to the campfire for more tinder.

They've all made two or three trips and the signal fires are just starting to take off when they get the first glimpse of the plane. It looks high above them ... too high. Its underbelly is red without any visible floats.

"Here!" Hunter screams.

Sam looks over at her brother to discover he's waving two burning sticks over his head. After throwing her supply of tire rubber on the now-intense flames of her fire, she picks one stick out with her good hand and begins running around with it. Their only hope is that it's still dark enough for the glow to stand out. If the lights are moving, it might actually draw the attention of someone on the plane. Assuming they're looking down.

"They *have* to see us," Ally cries. Snatching a flaming torch from John's fire, she joins the others in their wild racing around the clearing.

"Oh, my gosh. They're leaving!" Cassy has stopped in the middle of the glen, tears beginning to stream down her dirty face. "They didn't see us. What are we going to do?"

Sam stands beside her friend, bent over and gasping, as the plane continues past them without hesitation. Dark smoke is finally starting to spew up into the sky, but it may be too late. The worst part is that they don't have any more of the rubber strips left. They'll have to try to find something else that will burn black.

"Was that the search plane?" Ally throws her stick back onto one of the fires and wipes at her face. Her freckles stand out against her pale skin in the morning light, her red hair a wild tumble of tousled curls. "I just … want …. to go home!" Hiccupping around the sob in her throat, Ally collapses in the damp grass and wraps her arms around Rocky when he approaches her. Burying her face in his cinnamon colored fur, her shoulders heave as she cries in disappointment.

"No!" Hunter bellows, unwilling to give up. "Come back!" Dropping one of his sticks that burned out, he picks up another fully engulfed one. At risk of setting himself on fire, he runs heedlessly after the plane, up the slope towards the rocky peak.

"Hunter!" John scrambles after his friend, but before he can reach him, the sound of the plane changes. Stopping, he looks back up towards the sky.

Sam notices the fluctuation in the engine, too. Grabbing at Cassy's arm, she points. "Look!" As the plane begins to turn into a broad arch, the rising sun glints off the top of the silver wings. "It's coming back!"

Ever so slowly, the five of them watch in dazed relief as the pilot tips the wings back and forth in a wave of acknowledgement.

They're going home.

21

REUNITED

"**S**am! Sam, tell your story about Taquka-aq again. My sister hasn't heard it yet."

Sam grins at the young Tlingit girl standing eagerly in front her, her even younger sister in tow. The grizzly encounter has rapidly spread around the village and is already being treated like a new tribal legend.

The community center is full of people arriving from all corners of the fishing village. They've brought heaps of food for a grand celebration in recognition of the children's safe return, and Tulock's rescue.

The coordinates they provided led to a quick discovery of his and Kerry's location. According to the rescue pilot, Tulock was in very serious condition. They've been waiting for nearly two hours to hear on his prognosis from the nearest hospital.

Sam's eyes well with tears at the thought of Tulock. She's surprised she even has any tears left. Turning her head, she leans into her mother's shoulder. A protective arm wraps around her, and Sam is reminded of how many times she longed for this feeling of safety over the past seventy-two hours.

Her parents, Ally and John's parents, and Lisa were all keeping vigil from this room for the past three days. Sam's dad had them flown here immediately upon learning of the planes disappearance. They've been reluctant to let any of them out of their sight since the initial reunion.

"I think that maybe Sam needs a small break from her story," Kathy Wolf says gently to the girl still patiently waiting.

Sam straightens when she sees Ally making her way across the room, obviously brimming with exciting news. Distracted, Sam tries to break off the encounter before her friend gets to her. "Why don't I tell it again when everyone is done eating?"

Her face falls at Sam's offer and the young villager starts to turn away.

Sam stops the girl from leaving. "You can work on gathering everyone who hasn't heard it, and arrange a spot for them to sit."

Brightening at the suggestion, she immediately begins planning with her sister, mumbling about who they can talk to and where they will put the chairs.

Glad to have that settled, Sam turns to Ally as she gestures wildly at her with her hands. "The pilot is on the radio! Hurry, he's giving an update on Tulock!"

Not waiting for a reply, Ally pulls Sam out of her seat and they wave for the rest of their friends to join them as they run back to the radio room. A more reliable form of communication there than cell phones, the radio room is used to contact the mainland in case of emergencies.

Sam's dad is already there, and he turns to greet them as they enter. "He's going to be okay!" he announces, smiling broadly. He's developed some close friendships in the months he's lived in the village, and it turns out that

Tulock is one of them. He hasn't left the small room since the plane went out to retrieve his friend.

A loud cheer goes up from the five kids and is quickly joined by the rest of the gathered crowd as the message spreads.

The village Chief raises his arms and speaks loud enough for everyone to hear. "You are heroes."

Sam is surprised by the Chief's proclamation, but when she looks around at the handful of people gathered in the radio room, it's clear that he's talking to them.

"We only did what had to be done, sir," John replies.

"Maybe so," the wise man says slowly. "But sometimes it takes courage to act. Most would have chosen to stay where it felt safe, even though it may have been false. For that, our village will always be thankful." Turning to Sam's father, he extends a hand. "And you will always be welcome to fish beside us. Taquka-aq has spoken."

Though dressed in normal attire, the Chief has a powerful presence. As Ethan Wolf takes the offered hand, it is done with honor.

Her heart brimming with happiness, Sam seeks out the one other person there that intrigues her even more than the Chief. Auka. She is standing off to the side, holding the old leather ledger close to her chest. At seventy-eight, her long black hair is streaked with white. Although her face is lined by the ravages of time, she is still hauntingly beautiful. Walking nimbly across the room, she stops in front of Sam.

"Come." Without further direction, she turns and exits through a set of French doors and onto a back deck.

After the initial frenzied reunion with their parents, John asked the Chief if Auka was able to join them to hear the story of their plight on the mountain. When it came to the scene in the cave, he awkwardly gave her the ledger, unsure if what to say. Accepting it without a word, she left before they had a chance to talk with her about it.

Sam glances nervously at Ally. What if she's upset with them for finding the cave and removing the ledger? Taking her hand, Ally gives it an encouraging squeeze.

John is the first to follow, and then the rest

of them file out onto the large deck. It faces east, and the scenery is enough to take their breath away. With the ocean behind them, they're surrounded by a lush rainforest, the Alaska Boundary Range rising up to cut a sharp line through the sky in front of them. The peak of Shadow Mountain is visible, a reminder of how far they've come.

"Ben was always a mysterious man." Auka speaks the words tenderly.

Moving up to a spot near her at the railing, Sam watches as a bald eagle soars in lazy circles overhead.

Removing the piece of bark from the book, Auka finally turns to face them. "This is the mark he speaks of?"

"Yes, Ma'am," John answers. "I cut that off the last tree before the cave, so that you can choose whether to keep its location to yourself."

Nodding in approval, Auka grins and then carefully places the bark on the railing, running her fingers gently along the carving while remembering the past.

Digging into her jeans pocket, Sam pulls out the necklace. Holding her breath, she sets it on top of the wood.

Gasping, Auka's fingers linger over the locket, as if she's afraid it will disappear when she touches it. "Was this?" Looking up at Sam, she's unable to finish the question.

"Yes," Sam answers. "It was … with Ben."

Her hands shaking now, Auka manages to open the clasp. Overcome with emotion, she bows her head and holds the photo to her forehead, eyes closed.

"Will you try to find the gold?" Ally asks after several minutes have passed.

Shaking her head silently, Auka open her eyes and turns to stare at each of them in turn, ending with Sam.

"I don't think the gold is meant to be found," Sam says softly, returning the gaze.

"What makes you say that, child?" Auka questions, a small smile playing across her lips.

Shrugging, Sam looks to the mountains behind the village. Lifting her face up to the jagged peaks, she contemplates her response carefully before answering. "Some things are exactly where they were always meant to be. That gold is a part of Shadow Mountain. It's at the heart of it."

Auka joins her at the railing and they continue to watch the growing sunset together in silence.

"Will you bring Ben down?" Sam finally asks.

"No. Some things are exactly where they're meant to be."

Reaching out, Sam takes Auka's wrinkled hand in her own.

As Ally, Cassy, Hunter and John join them, a loud roar suddenly crashes through the silence of the twilight.

Instantly recognizing the sound, Sam spots a large shadow rising up on the nearest crest. Pawing the air, the colossal Kodiak bellows again. It bounces off the mountains behind it before echoing across the water and surrounding the village. Then, giving one last shake of its massive head, Taquka-aq lumbers back into the wilds of Shadow Mountain.

THE END

If you've enjoyed The Legend of Shadow Mountain, be sure to leave a review and check out the rest of The Samantha Wolf Series!

ABOUT THE AUTHOR

Tara Ellis, an Amazon bestselling author, lives in a small rural town in Washington State set in the beautiful Pacific Northwest. She enjoys the quiet lifestyle with her two kids and several dogs. Tara was a firefighter/EMT, and worked in the medical field for many years, before committing herself to writing young adult and middle grade novels full-time.

Visit her author page on Amazon to find all of her books!

amazon.com/author/taraellis

Made in the USA
San Bernardino, CA
12 November 2017